The Journey Prize Anthology

Winners of the $10,000 Journey Prize

1989
Holley Rubinsky (of Toronto, Ont., and Kaslo, B.C.)
for "Rapid Transits"

1990
Cynthia Flood (of Vancouver, B.C.)
for "My Father Took a Cake to France"

1991
Yann Martel (of Montreal, Que.)
for "The Facts Behind the Helsinki Roccamatios"

1992
Rozena Maart (of Ottawa, Ont.)
for "No Rosa, No District Six"

1993
Gayla Reid (of Vancouver, B.C.)
for "Sister Doyle's Men"

1994
Melissa Hardy (of London, Ont.)
for "Long Man the River"

1995
Kathryn Woodward (of Vancouver, B.C.)
for "Of Marranos and Gilded Angels"

The Journey Prize Anthology

Short Fiction from the Best of
Canada's New Writers

Selected with Olive Senior

M&S

Canadian Cataloguing in Publication Data

The National Library of Canada has catalogued this publication as follows:

Main entry under title:

The Journey Prize anthology:
the best short fiction from Canada's literary journals

Annual.
1–
Subtitle varies.
ISSN 1197-0693
ISBN 0-7710-4427-5 (v.8)

1. Short stories, Canadian (English).*
2. Canadian fiction (English) – 20th century.*

PS8329.J68   C813'.0108054   C93-039053-9
PR9197.32.J68

Typesetting by M&S

Printed and bound in Canada on acid-free paper.

The publishers acknowledge the support of the Canada Council and the
Ontario Arts Council for their publishing program.

"Bones" © Danuta Gleed; "Can You Wave Bye Bye, Baby?" © Elyse Gasco;
"Dental Bytes" © Rick Bowers; "Dust" © Alma Subasic; "Egypt Land"
© K.D. Miller; "The Friend" © Elizabeth Hay; "How I Crossed Over"
© David Elias; "Lessons from the Sputnik Diner" © Rick Maddocks;
"Monster Gaps" © Gregor Robinson; "Steam" © Murray Logan; "Turning
the Worm" © Linda Holeman; "The Winner's Circle" © Elaine Littman.
These stories are reprinted with permission of the authors.

McClelland & Stewart Inc.
The Canadian Publishers
481 University Avenue
Toronto, Ontario
M5G 2E9

1 2 3 4 5   00 99 98 97 96

About the Journey Prize Anthology

The $10,000 Journey Prize is awarded annually to a new and developing writer of distinction. This award, now in its eighth year, is made possible by James A. Michener's generous donation of his Canadian royalty earnings from his novel *Journey*, published by McClelland & Stewart Inc. in 1988. The winner of this year's Journey Prize, to be selected from among the twelve stories in this book, will be announced in October 1996 in Toronto as part of the International Festival of Authors.

The Journey Prize Anthology comprises a selection from submissions made by literary journals across Canada, and, in recognition of the vital role journals play in discovering new writers, McClelland & Stewart makes its own award of $2,000 to the journal that has submitted the winning entry.

This year's cover design is by student Edmund Li, and was selected through a competition held with the Ontario College of Art's third-year design class.

The Journey Prize Anthology has established itself as one of the most prestigious in the country. The anthology has become a who's who of up-and-coming writers, and many of the authors whose early work has appeared in the anthology's pages have gone on to single themselves out with collections of short stories and literary awards. The Journey Prize itself is the most significant monetary award given in Canada to a writer at the beginning of his or her career for a short story or excerpt from a longer fiction work in progress.

McClelland & Stewart would like to acknowledge the continuing enthusiastic support of writers, literary journal editors, and the public in the common celebration of the emergence of new voices in Canadian fiction.

Contents

DANUTA GLEED

Bones

Anna wraps the watercolour in a shiny paper striped pink and silver. She plants a pink bow, round and wide as a grapefruit, on top. She plans to carry it as hand luggage tomorrow, to keep it safe and to protect the wrapping from getting crushed. This painting pleases her; the waves brushed by a silver light, the red stains in the foreground, and, in the centre, a splatter of yellow, a point at which the sun may have recently set or where something – or someone – has fallen. A half-moon, transparent as a fingernail, sits in the top left-hand corner. On the bottom, centre, she has printed *Sunset*, so Janet, her mother, for whom the gift is intended, will at least have an idea.

"Happy birthday," Anna will murmur as she holds out the gift. The wrapping paper, the bow, are things Janet is sure to admire. She'll trace the bow with a short, red-tipped fingernail, thoughtfully, while Anna peers into the 'fridge for celery, green peppers, carrots, sour cream and packets of leek and onion soup for the dips. Bill, Anna's stepfather, will be clattering about outside with the barbecue, the chairs and tables for the birthday celebration, and when Anna turns around, Janet's eyes will be dark in her white face.

Anna is sure of this. She has become quite the expert.

~

Soon after her impulsive move to the west coast five years ago, Anna's paintings began to emerge quickly, one barely completed before another took shape. Like snapshots. Back east, she struggled over pictures of gardens crammed with sunflowers, slender white lilies and fat roses. She painted robins and blue-jays, small children in yellow bonnets building castles on the beach, a sun as round and sweet as an orange spinning in the sky. Everything light, bright, so perfect.

Now, in her studio apartment on the top floor of a creaky house, she stares at each completed watercolour in wonder, as if she doesn't know what she has painted or whether she has, indeed, painted it herself. She thinks about this development at times. Distance, she assumes, has somehow shifted her perspective. Or has she been hypnotized by the sharp air, the mountains, the ocean? Or the sunlight that fills the skylight on clear days? On dull days, raindrops race across. Some nights, the skylight is flooded with stars. But she doesn't care too much about the answer. And why, she asks herself, as long as the paintings keep coming, should she?

The first painting emerged within two days of her arrival, while boxes and suitcases were still stacked against the wall. Leafless, crooked black trees emerged beneath her brush, trapped in a cold blue and white fog. There was a figure, or a shadow, beyond the trees.

Winter, she printed at the bottom of the painting when it was completed. She sat back. Well, she whispered. Well.

Winter was the first painting Anna presented to Janet as a birthday gift. Next year there was *Water*. *Fire*, *Night Sky* followed. All have disappeared. When Anna asks about them, Janet claims she has packed them in boxes and stored them in a dark, dry spot in the basement to keep them safe. They may be valuable one day, she adds as she stares at Anna in a bemused way.

"Have you ever thought of painting something different?" she asks. "Something bright and cheerful. You know, like the stuff you did before?"

Anna pretends to think this question over.

In Janet's and Bill's house framed yellow and orange blooms hang above the living room fireplace. A cluster of white sail-boats skims across a too-blue lake above the sideboard. A young girl with yellow ribbons in her hair and lace around her collar sits inside an ornate golden frame in the hall.

Janet's question does not offend Anna. She sees it instead as proof that though Janet feigns indifference, the dark colours and odd, vague shapes she paints do disturb her. This makes Anna smile.

"All I do is reproduce the recurring images that appear in my head," she replies. She spreads her hands in a gesture that could pass for helplessness and adds, "And it happens to be a lucky coincidence that people open their wallets wide for them."

"Modern art," Janet sighs. "I'll never understand it."

～

Anna draws the curtains, slips into her nightdress. Tickets, gift, clothes for tomorrow, book for the plane, she counts in her head. In the kitchen, she pours the orange juice and milk down the drain. She moves to the living room, picks up the paper that has been lying on the table all day, smooths it, reads for the tenth or twentieth time the brief article squeezed into a corner of the back page.

MAN CARRIES HUMAN BONES IN SUITCASE

A thirty-three-year-old man from India was stopped by security guards at the airport in Tel Aviv when an X-ray machine revealed he was carrying items in his suitcase that were first believed to be weapons. On closer examination, the suitcase was found to contain a complete human skeleton. The man claimed that these were the bones of his father. He intended to keep travelling with them until he found a suitable place to settle, he explained. He then planned to bury his father nearby. Authorities are investigating.

Anna cuts out the article, slips it into her wallet. From the moment she first read it, she has wanted to know what has *not* been reported. She wants to know *why* and *how*. Did this man have some special bond with his father or did he feel guilt for something he did – or omitted to do? And how did he get the bones in the first place? Did he dig up his father's grave? Or worse? How much worse could it be?

She imagines again the shocked faces of the security guards, the agitation of this man, this son, as he fiddles with the locks on the suitcase. Drops of sweat the size of pinheads gather above his top lip. Damp hair sticks to his forehead. Because of some petty rule or regulation, the father he has tucked away for safe-keeping may now be taken from him. His hands begin to shake and he turns, to look for help.

People gather, stare. When the suitcase is finally flung open, they whisper, smirk their embarrassment and horror behind their hands.

Anna is certain that had she been there, she would have smiled her support at the man. She would have cheered him on because at least this devoted – or foolish – son knows something important. He knows where his father is, which is something she has not known about her own father for years. Twenty-five years, precisely.

All *she* knows is that her father is somewhere. Dead or alive, he is somewhere. Because even the dead take up space.

There are times when Anna thinks she makes her father up, conjures him up the way a magician pulls a rabbit from an empty hat, a row of coloured squares of fabric from his sleeve. But when she turns to the one photograph she has – proof – which now stands on a table by the window, next to a pot of purple African violets, she knows.

In the photograph, her father has a smooth face and dark eyes. He is wearing a uniform; baggy pants tucked into boots up to his ankles, a shirt that appears to be made of rough cloth, a flat cap cocked sideways on his head. The shirt has a collar so high it seems to be choking him. When Anna was a girl, her father pointed out to her the brass buttons on the shirt, the new, polished boots. And he shook his head as he told her he was proud the day the photograph was taken. He was a man, a sol-dier. He strutted about in his uniform and his parents, his younger brothers and sisters, laughed and clapped. He was off to war, to save them.

But when Anna looks at the photograph now she can't see the man or the soldier. She sees only the stunned eyes of a boy. A boy who must pretend to be a man, so he can pretend to be a soldier.

She splashes water over her face, brushes her teeth, runs a

comb through her hair. Quickly, quickly. If she stands in front of the mirror too long, she begins to see her father's pale face taking shape in the halo of her own black hair. Blank eyes, waxy skin, thinned lips. Dark eyes. The image blurs, recedes.

A trick of the light, but that cannot be all. She is getting older and her features are settling into his. She is forty, the same age her father was when he disappeared. She lifts a single white hair among the black, twirls and twirls it around her forefinger.

She will pass smoothly through airport security tomorrow. There is nothing suspicious in her suitcase or the canvas bag in which she will carry the watercolour, nothing startling or offensive.

The X-ray machine will pick up the metal frame of the picture in the bag. The bag will be unzipped, the gift removed. Probing fingers will run around the frame, lift the edge of the wrapping paper, gently, so as not to tear it. A nod, a glance at the solemn, dark-haired woman in sandals and loose cotton dress, and the gift will be returned.

Anna will smile as she picks up her bag. No one could possibly mistake a gift wrapped in pink and silver paper and topped with a pink bow for a weapon.

~

Another Friday night at seven, and Stefan, Anna's father, pats his pockets for cigarettes and wallet, grabs his jacket from the hook behind the door. There's the crunch of a car on the gravel beside the cottage as he leaves, the slam of doors, footsteps, raised voices, laughter. Janet's sisters – Betty and Sue – enter, faces half-hidden behind bags of groceries.

"Here." They thrust the bags at Anna.

Janet prepares coffee, lays out plates for cake and cookies. A bottle of sherry appears.

The women settle around the table. They are broad and tall, their heads wild with pale curls. Their faces are pink, as if they have been scrubbed recently. They sit with thighs apart, broad feet planted on the floor, grip mugs and glasses with firm hands. They talk about the weather, who will make or bring what for

Janet's birthday barbecue on Sunday, the price of eggs or milk, the new kind of food mixer Betty bought at Sears, and, eventually, they talk about Stefan.

Anna places milk, butter, juice, in the 'fridge. Tuna, cookies, cans of soup go in the top cupboard. She slams the cans down hard to drown out the sound of her father's name snagged in the voices behind her. Stefan. Stefan. Drinking again. Another job lost. Down to odd jobs now. Hardly enough to keep body and soul together. He'll never change and you, Janet, will never have a home of your own. You'll be stuck in this miserable family cottage forever.

Betty and Sue remind Janet they had warned her about those DPs who flooded the country after the war. They were not romantic or mysterious, as she wanted to believe.a They were strange. That's all. Anyone could see that. Hollow-cheeked, in loose clothes scavenged from somewhere, the women in flat brown shoes and black headscarves, they prowled the streets, peered into store windows, into passing faces, as if they were starving.

"Oh, but there were good times," Janet interrupts. "At his friends' in the evening, a bottle of vodka passed around – I got to quite like it. We sat on crates, lit candles, smoked, talked. They sang, wonderful songs. I didn't understand the words but, you know, they sounded like hymns."

"Dirges," Sue scoffs.

"And Stefan," Janet continues, her voice firm, "Stefan brought me chocolates or, when he was broke, wild flowers. Those dark eyes – I swear he bewitched me. And how could I not feel sorry for him? Every single member of his family died of disease or starvation in that labour camp in Siberia the Russians dragged them to. Imagine. He cried when he told me. Every single one – parents, sisters, brothers. He was in the army then – he doesn't even know where they were buried. Must have been awful."

"It may be a horrible thing to say, but it might have been better all round if he had gone too," Betty interrupts. There's a hush, the scrape of a chair. "Well, would you want to live if your whole family had gone? I wouldn't."

Anna is kneeling on the counter, arranging cereal boxes in the top cupboard. She pauses, waiting for her mother's voice. She glances over her shoulder. Janet is twisting her glass between two fingers, staring into it as if she can see something significant inside.

Anna folds the bags and slips them into the drawer.

"Good-night. Good-night." She kisses each aunt on the cheek.

"A bit early for bed, isn't it?" Sue asks.

"I'm going to read."

Anna sits on the bed in her narrow room and stares at her reflection in the mirror. She wonders where her father is. He won't tell her where he goes on Friday nights from seven until eleven. He pats her on the head when she asks and tells her not to worry.

The voices of the women press in through the walls. How sure they always sound, Anna thinks. How certain they are right. They make firm comments about everything – politicians, the state of the country, the state of the world. And people. "She has her father's nose, her mother's eyes," they say, as if a person is made up of puzzle pieces. "A high forehead, definitely his grandmother's." The sister's comments about Stefan are made in louder, more confident voices. They could be doctors making a diagnosis.

Anna leans towards the mirror. Her father's eyes, brown beads, stare back. Her hair is black, her face pale and long like his. Mysterious, romantic. There is nothing of Janet in her, she realizes with satisfaction.

Ignore him, Janet had said one winter night as she sat over her embroidery, fashioning a garden of roses on the hem of a skirt while Stefan tramped outside through the snow in his slippers.

"He's upset," Anna sobbed. "He'll freeze to death. We have to do something."

"He just wants attention." Janet snapped a thread with her teeth, a small, tight sound. "I can only stand so much, you know."

Anna grabbed her coat, pulled on her boots and ran to the

door. The cold pinched her face. Stefan was plodding through
snow that reached to his knees, shirt sleeves rolled up, arms
raised.

"Siberia! Siberia!" he yelled. "Bloody Siberia!" The words
sliced the night.

Well, Anna thought as she took his hand and led him back
as if he were an obedient child. Well, she murmured. It could be
Siberia, wherever, whatever it is. It's only a name, after all.
Who has the right to say it's not?

"Let's go," Stefan says to Anna late next day, the day before
the birthday barbecue.

She rouses herself from the grass where she's flipping through
a magazine. Her father slips a bottle into his pocket and
marches ahead. She walks behind, swinging her arms. She
hums as she watches Stefan's long strides. On days like this,
she's sure he knows everything.

They veer off the path and tramp through bushes and trees.
They stop, listen to the mutter of birds, squirrels, chipmunks.
Stefan pulls out the bottle from his pocket, raises it high, a
salute to the setting sun, and brings it to his lips.

"One day," he says, "I'll show you how to fish – in a proper
lake, not this filthy river. I'll teach you which grzyby – mushrooms – are poisonous and which are not."

He parts long grass with a stick. He is looking for szczaw – a
name he frowns over because he's unable to translate it. Green
leaves, he explains, a bit like dandelion leaves.

"We made szczaw soup at home," he tells Anna. "It's wonderful. A bit sour, a bit sweet. It's good to know about these
things in case you're stuck."

He grabs fistfuls of wild flowers; purple–blue harebells,
Queen Anne's lace, tall daisies. "They'll look fine on the picnic
table at the barbecue tomorrow," he says.

Janet is a shadow bending over the vegetable garden when
they return. She rises, holds out a tomato punctured with holes
and shakes her head.

Stefan thrusts the flowers towards her. "For you."

"Ah, Stefan. I can't cook these for dinner, now, can I? Can I?"
she cries. She drops the flowers on the picnic table and runs into

the cottage. They can see her in the kitchen window, a still silhouette in the light.

Stefan settles down on the dock. The sky is darkening. Anna lowers herself beside him. He extends his hand towards the river, a benediction. The water is a dark, rippled skin. He points to the stars that are boring pinpricks of light in the sky.

"And over there." He indicates a bright, steady glow. "A planet."

"Look at the moon," he says. "So round and smug. It's been there forever. When we're gone it will still be there. That moon face sees everything. Sits and watches. Little things, big things. The white rabbit-tail that flits under a bush. The petals of a flower closing for the night. The man who brandishes a gun, a knife. Today. Yesterday, last year. One hundred, one thousand years ago."

Anna looks up. The moon's face is still and solemn as a face on a coin. Stefan lifts his bottle to his lips. A frog croaks in the reeds. A breeze in a hurry rattles the leaves on the trees.

"There's no difference between the past and the present when the past is still going on in your head," Stefan says. He turns to Anna, his face white in the dusk. "You must never forget. You won't forget, will you? Promise me."

"No." Anna makes her voice firm. "No. I won't forget." She nods as she speaks because she wants him to know she is listening and that she wants to understand. Her bare feet slap the water. She wonders if he's joking and if she should laugh a little.

"Do you realize," Janet says to no one in particular at the barbecue next day, "that in two years I'll be forty? Forty! Half my life frittered away and nothing to show for it."

Anna notices Betty and Sue exchange glances with their husbands. Janet places a slice of chocolate cake in front of Stefan. He lets his fork clatter onto the plate, rises and strolls towards the bush, his hands in his pockets.

"We'll clear up," Betty says as soon as everyone has finished. Sue is already stacking the plates.

Anna takes Stefan's cake into the cottage, covers it with plastic wrap and leaves it in the 'fridge. Janet disappears into *the bedroom, emerges with a suitcase as Anna is washing the last bowl in the sink.*

"Come on." She grips Anna's wrist.

"Where to?"

"To Betty's. For a few days. Just you and me."

"What for?"

"I'll explain in the car."

"You go. I want to stay here."

"Anna. You must come." Janet points towards the bush. "It's for his own good. He needs to sort himself out."

Anna rubs a towel slowly between each finger while she thinks. Aunt Betty has a bungalow with a round swimming pool in the back yard. She has a bicycle Anna is allowed to use whenever she visits and a TV in the living room and the spare bedroom.

Anna hangs the towel slowly on a hook.

"Can we come back soon to see if everything is all right?" she asks.

Janet nods.

The first day, Anna takes her aunt's bicycle and cycles until her legs ache. She meets the girl across the road when she returns and invites her for a swim. Each morning they swim then watch the soaps in the afternoon. They swoon and giggle when their favourite actor appears.

When they have been at Betty's for ten days, Anna decides she doesn't want to see the girl across the road any more. She's too tired. She changes into her swimsuit and swims round and round the pool alone. She imagines she's a goldfish and the thought makes her laugh and cry at the same time.

She makes Janet promise they'll drop in at the cottage on the weekend. Janet laughs, pats her hair. "Sure, why not?" she replies, and adds that she's been offered a job in the cosmetics section of a department store. She starts in two weeks and needs to shop for decent clothes, make-up. She plans to have her hair done like this, she says, and thrusts a magazine at Anna. The woman in the magazine has smooth blonde hair piled high on her head. She is smiling, showing hard, white teeth.

On Saturday afternoon, Janet borrows Betty's car and drives to the cottage with Anna. The front door is locked. The back door gapes open.

Anna checks each room, each closet and cupboard. She opens the 'fridge and pulls out a plate holding a slice of chocolate cake.

Janet phones her family, checks with neighbours and calls the police. Anna sits on the doorstep until the sun drops behind the trees.

Day after day, frogmen slide into the water, emerge dripping, glisten in the sun like alien beings. They sit on the dock between dives and drink soft drinks from cans. They bring up a grey raincoat with a tear on the right sleeve, then a faded pink running shoe, a tartan scarf, and a long-sleeved checked shirt with black stains. Janet shakes her head each time.

"That's it," she says when they bring up a worn brown shoe late one afternoon. She turns it over. "That hole – he never had it fixed. That's it."

The police express regrets but, after six days, feel that continuing the search would be futile.

Janet builds a bonfire when they leave. She drags out Stefan's books, clothes, photographs, and hurls them onto the flames. Anna snatches the photograph of her father from the living room wall and hides it in her closet, behind her boots. She watches Janet from the back door. She grips the door frame so hard her fingers hurt. Flames snap and spit. Janet flickers dark and light as she raises her arms and lifts her face to the sky, as if she is dancing.

I'll never forgive you, Anna screams in her head. *Never, never, never.*

One year later Janet marries Bill, a red-faced widower with a pink scalp, her boss at the store. She wears a dress of multiple layers of thin, pale blue fabric at her wedding. There are small white daisies in her hair. Bill slips an arm around Janet's shoulders at the reception. She smiles into this face as she raises a glass of champagne.

"The past is past," she announces.

Bill and Janet live in a long white bungalow in a neighbourhood where streets are straight, lawns carpet-green. Clusters of pink and white begonias pack the flowerbeds beneath the front windows of their house. The walls inside are papered or painted with colours Janet calls citron, robin's egg blue, dusty rose. Silk roses, lilies, orchids fill each corner. There's a persistent sharp scent throughout the house which Anna has discovered emanates from the pretend lemons stuck in what look like egg cups hidden behind curtains, in drawers and closets. There is no mould, no rot, no dust, not one dark corner anywhere.

Every year, when Anna arrives for the birthday, Bill and Janet pick her up at the airport. Janet insists Anna sit in the front, beside Bill. She spreads herself in the back. She leans forward, taps Anna's shoulder as she talks. When they reach the road that runs parallel to the river, Anna forces herself to concentrate on Janet's voice, the tap tap of Janet's finger on her shoulder. The sun pushes through the window and she blinks. She tries to focus straight ahead, ignore patches of water that sparkle between buildings and trees.

But she cannot stop herself from turning, and she can't stop the tape that is always activated in her head. The old cottage is almost an hour's drive away, but who knows? *Maybe over there. Or over here.* A face wavers in the side window. Dark hair, dark eyes that glisten like glass. Skin so white it could be bone. She hears the croak of a frog. The night rustle of leaves. Low, slow words. *There's no difference between the past and the present when the past is still going on in your head.*

"Lovely," Janet murmurs when Anna presents the gift. Her red-tipped fingers slide over the bow, smooth the paper over and over. "Almost too pretty to open." Disappointment seeps from her voice, but she undoes the wrapping and turns to the window.

The sun slides through the glass and trickles through Janet's hair which she now keeps rusty red, the colour of a pomegranate. She removes the wrapping, tilts the painting this way and that, lowers it and stares at Anna as if she is looking for something, the small child, perhaps, who once scribbled ducks, a sun with wriggly rays, giant red and orange flowers, and people with lips turned up at the sides. Anna stares back. Janet's hands tremble. Flakes of powder are trapped in the folds of her skin. Her mouth creases into a pleat as she forces some approving sound from her lips.

And Anna remembers the woman with wild, pale curls, the smooth pink skin. Broad feet stomping through the vegetable garden. Firm hands plucking tomatoes and beans, yanking carrots. And suddenly she wants to place her fingers on Janet's arm. She wants to see Janet smile with pleasure and surprise. But she cannot make herself move. She is frozen, and the moment is lost.

At the birthday each year there are neighbours, friends old and new, Bill's and Janet's family. And the spare man, sometimes two. The spare man had a flat stomach once, a head of thick hair, and he talked with confidence – arrogance – about his ambitions, plans for his life. He parked a low, sleek car as close to the house as possible.

Now he is grey, balding, and his stomach is soft. Divorced – or widowed sometimes – he is eager to meet Janet's daughter, the artist, who's doing so well on the west coast. When Anna extends her hand, he holds it too long in his damp palm.

Anna smiles, excuses herself, brings out salads, pours soft drinks for the children. She slips from person to person, allocates each a portion of her time. Whenever she turns briefly to the spare man, Janet is there, in the corner of her eye, watching.

Dusk sweeps the garden. The children are querulous, their voices high, unreal. The adults, lethargic from too much food and drink, sink like soft dolls into the garden chairs.

Anna scoops up dishes and glasses.

"Stop," Janet shouts with mock horror. "Relax, have fun."

Anna shakes her head, carries on. The guests smile and Anna sees herself through their eyes. She is the good daughter, home for her mother's birthday, in her mother's garden, among family and her mother's friends. Everyone in the world is somewhere.

And some people are in two places at once. She is *here* and she is there on the dock, bare feet skimming the cool water. The river breeze tickles her skin. There's the roar of a lone motor boat, the slap slap of water against the dock. Silence. A sideways glance of the moon on black water. The clink of a bottle. A low, soft splash.

"Did you have a good time?" Janet asks when the guests have left.

"Very nice," Anna replies.

"Did you like anyone in particular?" Janet drags out plastic wrap as she speaks, stretches it over salads and cold cuts with intense concentration.

"Everyone was very nice."

"Friends and family. Aren't they wonderful?" Janet persists. "You're so far away," she adds, when Anna doesn't reply. "But you're happy out there, are you?"

Anna nods, scrapes leftovers into the garbage. Some day she will tell Janet something that will alarm her. She will tell her that it's not happiness she feels, exactly. She's more relieved than happy, which is a kind of happiness, in a way. When she opens her eyes on a day that is too bright, she is relieved to find herself alone so she can close her eyes again until the light is less intense. When she picks up a newspaper and reads about a baby found in a trash can, a car accident that destroyed a mother and father but left the child unharmed, or an article about a son who has been lost in a war he knew nothing about, she is relieved she can crumple the paper and throw it away.

Alone, she can flick the switch on the radio, change the channel on the TV. She can tread carefully, one deliberate step after another. She can look down to avoid holes, soft spots she may sink into. Relief, she figures, is far more important than love. It allows you to sleep at night.

~

Anna checks her wallet, her ticket again and stretches out on the bed. There are stars in the skylight tonight. Although she is not aware of being nervous, she wakes often the night before she flies, and when she does sleep, she always dreams the same dream. A plane somersaults in the sky. People tumble out, limbs spread. Magazines, dishes, plummet to the earth. Suitcases spill open. Shirts, pants, dresses, flap like sails. And tonight there will be bones. She is sure of this. Long white bones, gleaming as if polished. Small bones that clink in the void.

Her flight is at ten. She sets her alarm for five. The shapes have almost come together in her head and the outline will be ready before she leaves. Bones so luminous against the blackness, they hardly bear looking at. A skull, but not immediately recognizable as one. Positioned somewhere in the shadows, curtained by a cloud or a trickle of water thin as a silk scarf, to the left – or maybe to the right – of the canvas. Certainly not in the centre where a skull would be too obvious, too easy to dismiss as a gimmick, a cheap trick. And, at the bottom, a small, distorted figure trapped in the moon's icy light, arms extended, palms up.

RICK BOWERS

Dental Bytes

I can still see Dad, biting on bloodied handkerchiefs, begging us boys to brush our teeth and avoid his miserable fate, urging Mom to marry again after his death and be happy. His uppers had been pulled earlier that same afternoon while I struggled with fractions in math class, wished that I was old enough to drive and maybe take Miss Brimley out camping. A week before, Dad's lowers had been pried out of their sockets while I considered the fiery torment of Father Brébeuf in history class, wondered why Miss Brimley, always smiling in freshly coiffed hairdos, big blazers, and tight skirts above the knee, looked so much more beautiful than Mom. But looking back, I guess Miss Brimley was probably fifteen years younger than I am now. Mom was probably my age. Thirty-nine. Besides, Mom had me and Jim to contend with when she wasn't working at the snack bar. No wonder she looked used by the years, her face bitten in terseness as she rolled her eyes at my father's lamentations, told him to act like a man in front of his sons.

My abscessed bicuspid really pulsates up into my ear, pumping slowly with morbid significance. I look in the mirror and observe the swelling. My lower right mandible bulges out as if I were chewing a squash ball. But I don't really feel involved in the discomfort. I feel as though I were someone else observing me. Dad's ruined mouth, by contrast, must have felt pretty immediate to him: like an arm ripped off or an open sucking wound of the chest wall. His face looked crashed in. Furious in his distress until tired by his rigours, Dad moaned a couple of times through the night, inhaling deeply, muttering "Jesus, Jesus Christ almighty" in his sleep. Miss Brimley drew our attention to sucking wounds of the chest wall in health class once. She said we were to cover the site with a plastic bag or something and call an ambulance. I wanted so badly for her to demonstrate mouth-to-mouth artificial respiration on me. Miss Brimley's mouth was shapely, drawn into a full cherry-ripe smile with gorgeous red lips and white teeth. My lips are dry, my tongue a little shredded where I bit it under local anaesthetic. And now that the freezing is wearing off, my mouth throbs like a voice from the steaming dark. The codeine seems to rob me of emotional reaction, but the pain remains.

I don't usually live in a great deal of pain. I'm an associate professor of English, with full dental coverage, on study leave at 80 per cent of my salary. My work during sabbatical involves the cultural rehabilitation of Renaissance polymath Thomas Phaer, a physician, lawyer, MP, and general man of letters in sixteenth-century England. Big deal. Obscure. Nobody's life depends on it. But I guess my sabbatical project represents a further particle of knowledge to be contributed to the study of the humanities. No one else will do it if I don't. Oh, my aching head. Besides, I firmly believe that knowledge for its own sake is valuable. Such academic faith rescues me from more immediate and intolerable considerations: my childishness, my child*less*ness, my uncomfortable sense that life is rapidly passing me by as I twiddle my thumbs and envy the accomplishments of others. Some real pain comes as almost a relief, a reminder that there *is* a world elsewhere of involvement and interaction, a world where surprise can enter the heart like a pickaxe through the chest.

I observe my face in the mirror once more, bare my teeth and feel a jet in my mouth. The teeth themselves feel as though they have been chewing on tin foil. I watch my fingers explore along the whiskery ridge of my misshapen jaw, wonder at the pain of toothache prior to twentieth-century dentistry. In a section of his 1544 medical text titled "Breedynge of teeth," Phaer writes: "And wh[e]n the peyne is greatte and intollerable with aposteme or inflammation of the gommes, it is good to make an oynt-mente of oyle of roses with the juyce of morelle, otherwyse called nyghtshade." Roses and deadly nightshade – the ancients knew best how to appease pain and all its symbolism. They treated pain with the mercilessness of love. Today, we think we can counteract pain with drugs. I squeeze my eyes shut, and a hum of sad choirboys tunes up in the back of my head. Alto-tenors predominate. My tongue protrudes and I can see myself breathing on the mirror. It wearies me. I remember things.

In grade five, Miss Brimley always smiled at me. A girl-woman, tall and curvaceous, she used to put her hand on my shoulder during art class. "Use any colours you want, John," she said. "You have a flair for colours." The other teachers were trolls. Mom, by contrast, was a worn-out woman who didn't like colours all that much. She was always tight-lipped and angry about Dad, about the world. "Make you sick!" was her response to everything. "John, clean up that mess," she'd say. "Make you sick!" Or, "John, why did you have to go and do that? Make you sick!" On weekends, she'd sit back in her sofa chair, exhale cigarette smoke to the ceiling, complain to her friends: "Did you see the makeup she was wearing? Make you sick! And the colours . . . oh my!" Mom's friends all wore pants with zippered sides that never quite closed. They traded maga-zines back and forth, magazines that advertised a lot of bras. The back cover of the magazines always showed a man and woman dancing cheek-to-cheek. "To herself: He forgets I am 50." By now, somewhere, Miss Brimley is well over fifty years of age. I touch my swollen face, cupping the bulge of my jaw in the palm of my hand. I'll leave off shaving until tomorrow. Sometimes I really do feel sick.

Last night, I saw an advertisement on TV for a face cream that purported to "reverse the aging process." The model – fabulously blonde, slim-nosed, slight-waisted, and leggy under a luxurious blue terrycloth robe – held the product up to her face for a full-frame closeup and declared: "*You* have the choice." This was dur-ing a baseball broadcast, for God's sake. My choices, I feel, are severely limited. Interviewed on a syndicated talk show, fashion writer Angela Veno commented as follows: "A successful model need only be a standard size eight, five-foot-nine or over, have good skin and hair, and both front teeth." Her humour seems lame to me. I felt an ache in my jawline, reached for the channel selector, thought about more codeine. But then I froze as the commercial for the age-reversal cream was repeated. The model looked to be the spitting image of Loreena, my teenage sweetheart. Was there a technical slip-up? Was the commercial aimed at a male viewing audience? Dear God, was it aimed at me? I've got to get out more. Either that, or lose this aching tooth. My head feels as though it's closing. If I thought for a moment that reversal of the aging process was possible, I would buy stock in the company. As an associate professor, I make enough to do so. I'm fully insured, without children, on double income with my spouse, looking at mutual funds, and spending very little on entertainment. Pathetic.

Pain is relative and subjective. A threshold of emotionality is involved. Dr. Trudy Brydges, my dentist, inquired about the nature of my pain, urging me to specify whether it was a sharp, piercing, localized sensation or a more generalized dull, throbbing ache. This confused me momentarily. Using the hand mirror which she provided, I pointed daintily with my pinky finger at the howling tooth in question. She performed a percussion test, knocking against the specified tooth with the handle of a dental instrument. My head exploded. All confusion left me. Jagged spikes of purple and orange shot out of my ears into the waiting room where they overheard Paula, Dr. Trudy's receptionist, complaining about Greg. "He's such a baby," she said. My forehead ridged itself down my face. "Are you okay, John?" asked Trudy. I nodded, exhaling aromatic rocky boulders, my face rattling like a stack of sharpened tin forks. A whiff of iodine wobbled in my sinuses and I felt myself crawling up the back of the chair.

During recess once, while playing sidewalk soccer, I scraped my knee off. It oozed orange and red and it watered down my shin. Eyes closed, I sucked air that tasted like rust and crabapples. Miss Brimley asked me "Are you okay, John?" Her look of concern was as beautiful as her smile. She smiled fully at me. She placed both hands on my shoulders. Then she took me to the teachers' lounge, washed the grit out of my wound. "This iodine will sting you, John," she said. But I didn't mind so long as Miss Brimley was there, was speaking to me with sympathetic apprehension. In fact, I had never felt better in my life than I did right then, alone with Miss Brimley in the teachers' lounge, gritting my teeth, playing the brave soldier, living by her attentions. Miss Brimley placed a cold cloth on my forehead, told me to lean back on the couch, said that I could stay in the room as long as I liked until I felt better. I then remember sniffing a little in sweet torment as she sat with me, hugged me to her on the couch. She smelled like candy and flowers. Her body felt large and comforting and soft. She hummed a little, hushing me gently and assuring me that I would be all right. I clung to her, didn't risk moving a muscle in case it might lead to rearrangement or loss of contact.

Mr. Peacock, our surly principal, arrived a little later to drive me to the hospital in his car. His teeth were perpetually tobacco-stained and grimy. I never liked him. He jovially parted me and Miss Brimley, made light of my resistance. But he seemed genuinely concerned too, accompanying me to outpatients without comment. All I could think of, as my knee crusted over, was the special relationship between Miss Brimley and me. My eyes misted in remembrance of the smooth feel of her hand in my hair and around the back of my neck. Nobody else in class ever received such treatment. My pain was pleasure so long as I could close my eyes and see her smiling face.

The debonair Elizabethan courtier Sir Philip Sidney wrote a poem entitled "When His Lady Had Pain in Her Face," and it made me reflect upon Elizabethan dentistry and the pleasing pain of love in a sonneteer's mind. Love, love, the pain of love I seek. Hand me the pliers. This, just after Dr. Trudy's hygienist, Kayla, placed a book of Garfield cartoons on my lap. Concerned and well-meaning, Kayla offered, "Perhaps this will help a little?" Her every utterance is a tentative offering, her voice rising musically: "Hi. My name's Kayla? Looks like you're going to have . . . a root canal?" I feel cranky and doubtful. Garfield cartoons? I teach English literature at the university, goddammit. Not that I'd like to peruse essays on *Hamlet* in my current painful condition (although one or two of my more vaguely crazed colleagues probably would), but some form of reading matter above the grade five level would be welcome. When in grade five, I watched Miss Brimley's captivatingly fresh face and beautiful white teeth and was immune to everything else. I was better then.

Dad confided to me once that he never felt young again after he got his dentures. This was on the morning of my first communion. Just moments before, he had confessed his atheism to me as he knotted my necktie. I wondered to myself if dentures and loss of faith were somehow connected. Years later, a dentist in Hamilton, Ontario, checking me over for a possible stint with CUSO, complimented me on the general condition of my teeth. I told him that my mother always believed in the maxim "bad teeth, bad people." "Smart woman," he intoned without a trace of irony as he adjusted the lamp above my face. By then, I had privately amended Mom's line to "bad teeth, poor people," and felt certain that my dentist, with his red BMW and crisp Arrow shirts, must have had some notion of the economic side of the inequation. Even dental coverage proves expensive. A colleague of mine at the English Department once advised me, "Just think 'orthodontist' and be thankful that you and Beryl don't have any kids." She added that the very word "orthodontist" made her feel old. Bitten by her own mortality, I guess. That dentist back in Hamilton informed me as follows: "As we age, our gumlines recede and are subject to increased sensitivity." As we *age?* I heard it from him first.

But I first felt the weight of years when Beryl suggested that we entrust our dental health to Dr. Trudy. "Dr. Trudy Brydges," she said. "Everyone calls her 'Dr. Trudy.' She's really good, really informal, but really highly qualified too. Everyone at the office goes to her. Apparently she's connected to the Faculty of Dentistry at the university." Great. A colleague. In designer T-shirt and pleated pants, Dr. Trudy is a pleasant-looking professional woman. She looks like someone who might have refused to go out with me in graduate school. Not a bad recommendation really. But she's no older than Beryl and me. This

might give one pause momentarily, but what really crushes me
is the youth of her staff. Paula, working on her nails and talking
about Greg; Kayla, admiring Paula's outfits, humming along
with the easy listening music, wondering about redecorating;
Gail, looking through travel magazines, asking aloud, "Is there
really anything to do in Singapore?" These are pleasant, competent, but *young* women. I mention this to Beryl and she
accuses me of having a gender crisis. I assure her that the problem is age, not sex. She counters that for women sex and age are
always combined. Silenced again, I feel as though we have wandered off the original topic. And I don't feel good about it, in the
same way as I don't feel good about seeing roadkill.

At Dr. Trudy's, at 8 a.m., I made my way to The Chair. I'm on
penicillin, Tylenol 3, and a double scotch, and I don't feel good
about it.

Gail, Dr. Trudy's tall and confidently attractive assistant,
referred to the X-ray of my painful premolars and explained the
anatomy of a root canal. "It's real easy," she said. "Trudy drills
down through the original filling – it's a deep one, and there was
some exposed pulp – to get into the root itself, which will be
killed, hollowed out, and filled with a rubberized gutta-percha
amalgam. That's it."

"So what you're saying," I respond, reaching for some notion
of the relative pain involved, "is that the tooth itself will be
killed off but preserved within my mouth as its own sort of
false tooth?"

"That's right," Gail returned. "Think of it as your own little
denture."

She whisked away in white-uniformed swiftness, and I was
left to think. Dentures. All the professional hockey players wear
them. Team dentists in the NHL are treated like gods. I can see
again the toothless grins of Bobby Hull, Bobby Clarke, all the
great Bobbies. Bobby Orr, Bobby Baun, Bobby Rousseau, Bobby
Pulford, Bobby Schmautz, Bobby Carpenter, Bobby Smith – my
brother and I used to have all the hockey cards. Sickened by our
continual bickering over them, Dad threw the hockey cards out
the driver-side window of our 1968 Plymouth Fury somewhere
near Moncton, New Brunswick. They twisted and flew like

leaves in a storm through the air, in the ditches, and across the highway. I watched them through the rear window, felt as though my life was at an end. Jim didn't care. He crossed his arms silently with the spite of a younger brother. But the loss was near maddening to me. My face was on fire. I have always wanted to get back there around Moncton and check the local card shops.

Brother Jim got a tooth knocked out playing Junior B hockey. I used to wonder if the "B" stood for Bobby. He claims that his missing-tooth pirate smile attracted Linda to him. A physician in Halifax took some cartilage out of Jim's knee and he took on selling real estate full time. He and Linda married. Their wedding photos are populated by Jim's toothless hockey-playing chums in ill-fitting tuxedos. The wedding party looks ready for a gang fight. Two kids and four mortgages later, Jim took a course called "Improving Appearances," had a false tooth inserted, lost twenty pounds, washed away some grey, and upped his sales by 40 per cent. This was just last summer. I was back home visiting. Jim got Linda to take a picture of me and him together, smiling by the barbecue. Brothers.

Actually, Jim was doing all the smiling. I looked as though I had swallowed a mouthful of crooked pins. Linda held the picture up to the light. "John, I've never seen you looking so much like Dad as you do in this photo," she commented agreeably. Perhaps the age showed on my face. My adolescence had just ended. Precisely at that time, I felt as though I had taken multiple stab wounds in the lower belly. I had just got off the phone to my high school/university sweetheart, Loreena, who informed me that she had to decline my offer of lunch. "I don't think my husband would like that," she said with a little laugh. Then: "I don't know if I told you or not, John, that I'm married now." She hadn't. I didn't think she was exactly manless, but married? I felt a cold shower of lighter fluid in my veins. We hadn't really spoken for a year or two – we sent a postcard here and there – but she said that she and Scotty had now been married for over four years. "I don't think you've ever met him," she said. "He's really nice." I felt stupefied, orphaned, sunk – a prawn in the game of life.

Hot mercury welled up in my sinuses. I know a bit about

disappointment and embarrassment, but I have never felt so completely irrelevant. Academics can stand being uninformed, even being wrong. But to be so completely beside the point is to be in hell. Then a fizz of resentment kicked in. Loreena's cheery information hatched a nest of worms in my chest, and I could feel my teeth grinding.

When I was eighteen, my impacted wisdom teeth were cut out under general anaesthetic. Loreena lovingly drove me to the hospital. Stunned and weakened in the recovery room, I saw her and Mom standing together watching me. Mom's look of fierce concern penetrated me to the spine. She had taken the afternoon off from the snack bar without pay, and I felt as though I had come back from the dead only to realize that I was *her* baby. Loreena, fresh-faced in tightly fitting jeans and long curly blonde hair, was only a tolerable little friend compared to the deep, animal, unremunerated love of a mother. It made me feel uncomfortable. But it made me feel loved too. A student of mine named Bruce was urged by his physician father to forget about medical school and get into dentistry. "Work 9 to 5 and print your own money," he said. My own Dad, a driver for the P.E.I. Department of Highways, urged Jim and me to always support the union, to keep our mouths shut, and never to volunteer for anything – advice worthy of consideration.

I tried always to keep my mouth shut, to be "seen and not heard," as Dad liked to put it. A girl in my grade five class named Margie had gapped and pointy teeth and was taunted with the name "Gargoyle." Joyously hateful, they used to sing it at her: "*Gargoyle, Gargoyle / Eat a pot of hot oil!*" Over and over again – they seemed never to tire of it. Christ, where do kids come up with such mindless cruelty? I'm proud to say that I never chimed in with such grade-school wickedness. But my motives had more to do with self-preservation than virtue because my teeth were gapped and pointy too. I didn't dare show my teeth. My smiles were determinedly "lip" smiles, smiles that Miss Brimley once said seemed to hide more than they revealed. At the time, I was thinking how heavenly it would be if Miss Brimley were to give me a bath.

Miss Brimley's first name was Barb. I heard it from Mr. Mac-Donald the shop teacher. I didn't really know him. I was too young to take shop. But I was just arriving at the teachers' lounge one day to show Miss Brimley the paper Christmas tree ornament I had made when I saw him from behind as he placed his hand on her ample bum. "How ya doooin', Barb?" he drooled with a mock groan that I found curious. "Don't, Mac," she responded with a hurried little laugh, moving her shoulders and twisting around in protest. "Oh, hello, John," she said with a freshened smile when she saw me. Then before I could say a word she gently closed the door to the teachers' lounge in my face. I felt kicked in the head. I thought about how I'd like to get Mr. MacDonald's head between two bricks.

We moved away before I got to grade eight and could take shop. Our new dentist was Dr. Franz. A gentle giant with a thick and juicy German accent, he used to whisper "Mac oppen pleese" when he wanted us to open our mouths. Jim and I used to imitate his accent. I thought at the time that Dr. Franz meant "mouth" when he said "mac." And every time I heard him say "mac," I was bitterly reminded of Mr. MacDonald the shop teacher. I chewed my boyhood anguish. I now know that Dr. Franz, as a non-English speaker, was using the verb "make" and pronouncing it "mak." Such semantic realizations stand in for a good deal in English studies. As a colleague of mine once opined: "We are highly professional people, trained in the understanding of complex, closed systems of language and signification. Consequently, English grads are sought after by corporations that require critical and cultural expertise." Sounds good, but I don't imagine that a "closed system" such as NASA or IBM or Health and Welfare Canada is actively recruiting B.A.s in English. Of course, as in most things, I could be wrong.

Upon hearing that I teach English, Dr. Trudy told me that she started out in linguistics, moved on to speech pathology, and finally got so interested in the anatomy of it all that she ended up in dentistry school. "Sounds like something to really get your teeth into," I observed. She smiled in response, but it was not a nice smile. In fact, I had the distinct sense that I could hear flesh tearing somewhere. I felt like a lanced gumboil. A colleague of mine said that his dentist was an Oriental woman with extremely adept and tiny hands. Dr. Franz used to have hands as huge and hairy as buffalo heads. I felt like asking my colleague if his dentist with the micro hands required the use of dental instruments. Hand me the pliers.

Miss Brimley had beautiful hands, but she also had dentures. There, I said it. I wrote my pain. My stupid boyish vanity melted into my shorts as Miss Brimley pulled out her teeth and snapped them at me in a humorous attempt to cheer me up that morning in the teachers' lounge as my kneecap hung down on my shin. Her face crumpled and transformed into that of the witch in *Hansel and Gretel*, and she snapped her gums at me. The gesture was girlish, lighthearted, even somewhat daring for a young woman who so obviously cared about her features and their handsome presentation. But Miss Brimley didn't care. She used her sunken face as if it were a comic prop. She did it for me, to cheer me up. I think I nearly passed out. Unperturbed, however, and fast as a grin, she whipped her teeth back into her face just before Mr. Peacock arrived to take me to outpatients. She was beautiful again. But I was shaken to the roots of my petty boyhood desires.

That night, I considered Dad in his toothless anguish and connected it to the pain that Miss Brimley, as a denture wearer, must have had to endure. It made me love her even more. Dad used to scrape and groom and line and soak his dentures, trying always to discover a perfect fit and condition that always perfectly eluded him. My love life seems to have been lived in the same way. Beryl has Miss Brimley's hair, her smile too. But she doesn't have dentures. Neither does she have Miss Brimley's tight skirts or big round legs. She deceived me to the toes by having a tubal ligation without telling me. This was just before we finally moved in together. She told me about it three years later. "I did it for *us*," she insisted tearfully, her good face long and contorted in pain. Bludgeoned by her reasoning, I quietly acceded to our installation as a childless couple. Then I agreed a couple of years ago to the whole fertility-clinic yoga after Beryl had the operation reversed. And it all failed. Beryl is the woman of my adult life. I love her. But somewhere in the recesses of my boyhood R-brain I guess I'm still chasing past Beryl and Loreena, searching for Miss Brimley and her unselfish sense of care. Maybe I'm just searching for my fixated boyhood. It's basically a sordid sentimental search that craves the embrace of high but lost hopes. And I'm sure it's not at all uncommon. For me, that's over thirty years of searching now. At times, I wonder if my masochism has a limit. At other times I'm so full of regret that I chew my memories with the relish of an outed pedophile, a position which a few of my more vaguely crazed colleagues would probably applaud as both fully theorized and actively political.

My own root canal today must be smalltime compared to the pain that full denture wearers must have to endure. But Dr. Trudy, assisted by Gail, reduced me to a groaning pulp a couple of times with her drilling, probing, and syringing. She whirred through old decay, and a stench of electrocuted carcasses wafted up into my nostrils. I felt a crispy tanned vellum in my head, covered with obscene graffiti, crinkle itself into origami shapes of birds, and boxes, and precious stones. A gathering moan of restraint and distress welled up in my ears like a prison full of birthing mothers. Quietly unperturbed, Trudy and Gail worked on with tight-lipped effort. From time to time, they exchanged mathematical codes. They had my full attention. "How're you doing, John?" Trudy asked impassively. Laid out below her, my feet above my head, all I could do was nod and emit a positive little groan. I found myself moment-by-moment in isolation, pummelled, helplessly gagged by the rubbery, fubbery dental dam, disallowing any verbal response as Trudy and Gail continued on, absently chatting now about tourist sites in England, asking me how Beryl was doing with her t'ai chi classes. "You've got a nice long root, John," commented Trudy without emphasis as she explored my howling nerve with one of a series of pin-shaped files. She needn't have said. At that instant, I was feeling every harried micrometre of it in my head, out to the elevators, and all the way down to the street.

Afterwards, both Trudy and Gail accompanied me to the reception desk. They apologized profusely for the pain they had put me through, but I assured them through a codeine haze that

I understood it all to be nothing personal, just dentistry. They were soothing in their responses. Paula and Kayla joined in, asked if they should call a taxi for me. I declined, courteously spitting blood into a tissue. "Take some more," offered Paula, handing me a box the size of a footlocker. I felt as if I was swallowing a mixture of melted glass and spicy cologne.

Trudy's staff are all competent, professional young women deserving the respect and gratitude of their patients. I'm proud to count myself as one. If I had a daughter – and Beryl is talking more and more about adoption these days – I'd want her to work in Dr. Trudy's office, perhaps one day as her partner. It's good to have high hopes. But, to me, dental health and hopelessness seem to go well together. And my whole life so far has been lived hopelessly "after the fact." Before she told me about the tubal ligation, I used to actually pray that Beryl would get pregnant. Just before that last phone call to Loreena, I still entertained vague notions that she and I would somehow get together, maybe get married in later life after retirement. I realize now that I can't even form an accurate picture of Miss Brimley in my mind. God, I feel like an idiot. Perhaps if I could just get this offending tooth out of my head I might reclaim a few years. I need to do something to extricate myself. I've known it since I was a boy. It hurts. Someone, please, hand me the pliers.

ALMA SUBASIC

Dust

Pa sent me here, to the crazy-house, after Billy died. The police found him in my pa's barn, face mashed into straw, legs spread-eagled, his toes pointed inwards, hands balled up. He looked like he was passed out from drink but he was shot through four times: one bullet in his stomach, one in the chest, one in the shoulder and one in his dinger. That's why they figured I did it, but I wasn't the only gal Billy diddled.

There's a garden here with snapdragons that I tend. I like to put my fingers in their little mouths so they can bite me, soft bites like a newborn kitten's. All we ever grew at my pa's were rusty licence-plates and chain and bits of paper and cigarette butts. The soil was poor – so poor we didn't have grass. Our farm was like a poor, balding man. Pa's a poor, balding man kept moist with liquor. The soil's good here, though. Black and full of wriggling worms I can pull out like threads from an old sweater and mash between my fingers. Makes me feel alive.

I tend the garden when I don't feel so tired. I gotta keep busy so I don't go crazy.

I met Billy at the Blue Muzette. I was sitting with my friend Cass Bigelow who was chewing on her fingernails and spitting them on the floor of the diner. It embarrassed me but I didn't say nothing. I just listened to the small clicks her nails made hitting the floor. Cass was my best friend. Whenever pa was fit to scrap, she let me sleep on her sofa which smelled like her dog Mojo.

I didn't see Billy till he came up to me and Cass and said,
Whatcha pretty gals doin' on such a fine day?

Cass piped up: Whatcha think we're doin', honey, gettin' our
hair done for a strawberry supper? Billy put his hands on our
table and leaned into Cass, raising the muscles on his arms and
whispered,

Now, why you wanna get smart with me, you don't even
know me?

I know your kind, Billy Carstairs, blowin' through town like
a toronado leavin' gals all shook up. You just blow away now.
Billy didn't blow away. He looked at me and smiled the nicest
smile. I looked down at my hands.

You leave her alone now. Cass slapped Billy's arm. She ain't
so bright. You go pick on them city gals, they'll eat you alive.
Billy asked me what my name was and I told him. Next thing,
he was sitting beside me smelling of tobacco and sweat. He
asked me if I liked the movies and I said I'd only seen one,
Night of the Hunter, but that I'd enjoyed it. He asked me to go
out that Saturday night to see *Bonnie and Clyde* and I said yes
before I'd even thought the word. Cass spoke up. Leave her
alone, Billy. And I said, Cass, I know what I'm doing. I said that.
I know what I'm doing.

In the movie theatre, Billy put his hand between my legs, on my
boo-boo. I watched *Bonnie and Clyde* and thought about how
beautiful Warren Beatty was. Billy rubbed my boo-boo and it felt
nice and wet and warm. Swollen. When Billy put his finger
inside me it hurt but I didn't say nothing. He put my hand on his
dinger and he bucked against it. I unzipped his jeans, leaned over
to put my mouth around his dinger like Cass told me fellas
liked but Billy pushed my head away. Didn't gather me to him.
He was angry and I didn't know why. Just as I started to pull
away Billy pushed my head down on his dinger and it hit the
back of my throat. I choked and cried and wished it were all done
so I could just watch Warren Beatty. Once it was all over, I
couldn't concentrate on the movie for all the thoughts whirling
around in my head. Much as I wanted to run from Billy, the place
I'da run to was no escape.

Billy didn't see me all the way home. He left me in front of Agatha Bailey's cherry tree without saying good-night. I hurried to get in before pa woke up from his drunk. I smelled blood on me and knew I had to wash and change before pa knew I was home. The house was dark. I didn't hear nothing. I made sure not to creak the first stair or touch our rickety banister. My foot barely on the first stair, pa yelled, Who's the whore in my house? He said it loud, his hearing lost to drink. But his sense of smell is sharper than a bloodhound's and I knew he could smell the blood between my legs and the jism in the back of my throat.

I said is there a whorin' bitch in my house? Pa came out of the parlour with a belt in his hand and saw me at the stairwell. You girl? You bin whorin'?

No pa, I bin with Cass.

Bullshit! You bin whorin'! Now, lose them dancin' panties and bend over. I did as he asked. Whipping sure beat punching. I put my knees on the second stair and my hands on the third. I made sure not to wriggle or yelp because that made pa hit harder. The belt missed a few times, hit the stairs and raised dust. To make myself unmindful of pain, I stared at the dust. The moonlight streaming through the parlour window made it shine like millions of tiny glow worms.

A whore like your ma before ya. A whore plain and simple. He stopped hitting me after a time and stumbled back into the darkness dragging his belt behind him like a tail.

My brother Jim was laying on the ground with his lambs while I set my clothes out to dry. Pa didn't let Jim keep a dog because they ate too much. Shows you how little pa knows about the nature of lambs. Jim spent his days tending to his animals. Loving them. He asked me what I was doing and I said hanging my dancing pants to dry. He asked me if pa beat me the night before and I said yes. He said he was sorry, that pa beat him too. Pa beat Jim for being a sissy. Jim isn't like other fellas. He don't ping off birds or blow up frogs. He won't eat animals. That angers pa most. Pa figures meat eating proves we're superior to animals, Bible says so. Most of the time we didn't have to eat anything because by mid-supper pa's face'd fall into his food and he'd sleep for hours with his face mashed into his baked beans.

With freedom, Jim'd play his ukulele. I'd hug pictures of ma that pa hadn't busted up, and remember the swoosh of her skirt and the cinnamony smell of her bosom. Eventually, pa'd holler: What in hell time is it? Jesus, what the hell . . . and the ukulele and the pictures and Jim and me'd hide until morning, leaving pa to swear at the dark.

I met Cass at the Blue Muzette and she asked me about Billy and I told her about our courting and she said, My God, doesn't he know you ain't so bright? Honey, did he hurt you? I said, Cass, quit saying I ain't so bright. Stop repeatin' it like some prayer. Cass took elocution classes at Pritchard's School for Young Ladies and thought she was better than everybody else because of it. But I knew she'd spent time in the hoozgow for stealing a push-up bra from Carlson's Sundries. She stole it even though she had nothing to push up far as I could tell. Bobby Carlson stopped her as she walked out with it and said if Cass'd give him a suck he'd let her go. She sucked his dinger for a good hour in the back of the store with the blinds down and the door locked and customers yelping and hollering outside. But Bobby didn't let Cass go even after he'd unloaded. He called the police and Cass was put in the hoozgow overnight. That's the story I recall each time Cass says I ain't so bright.

On our second date, Billy pushed my face into the grass in the cemetery, shucked my underwear off and stuck his dinger into my rear. To make myself unmindful of pain, I thought of all the dead people under me and wondered how long it took to turn to dust once you were dead in the ground. Sometimes I wish I was dead, just dust getting blown around in a million different directions. It didn't take long for Billy to finish. I got up and jism ran down the insides of my legs. Billy lit a cigarette and walked away from me. I followed him, scratching an antbite on my right cheek, wondering how courting was for other girls.

One day, Jim asked me about Billy while he tended to his goats and lambs and rabbits. Jim's like a rabbit. His nostrils quiver and his eyes stare wide and nervous. He looks at you sidelong, never square in the eye. Even me, his own sister.

So what's he like, honey?

Oh, okay . . .

Is he nice?

Nice enough.

Well, does he treat you nice?

Sort of . . .

Honey, don't be wastin' your time with him if he ain't treatin' you nice. A boy ain't worth much if he ain't nice. Lord help ya, if your fella ain't nice.

Oh, he's nice. I didn't tell Jim much about me and Billy. Being with Billy sure beat living with pa. I didn't want to lose Billy for anything.

I have one friend here in the crazyhouse. Her name's Muguet Dupree. She's what they call autistic. At first, I thought she was here for being artistic, maybe some kind of mad painter who'd painted the town red once too often. Muguet rocks back and forth and doesn't say too much but she gives me pictures of the animals she draws: raccoons, squirrels and woodchucks. She draws them right down to their little whiskers. She rocks and stares at them as they scurry through the garden looking for food. I watch her and understand what can make a person so quiet, so untied to the universe, like a dying planet.

Billy didn't take much stock in the Bible except for the parts blaming women for the world's ills.

I surprised Billy on the riverbank one day. He was fishing with a homemade pole. I watched him for a while expecting him to behave in some way he wouldn't in front of me. He just sat still as the water in front of him. I stood behind him and covered his eyes with my hands.

Guess who, I asked.

Jesus H. Christ, you scared the hell out of me. Billy tugged my hands off his face. Don't you ever, ever come up behind me

again. That is about the worst thing you can do to a man, surprise him like that.

I didn't mean to scare you, Billy.

Sure ya did. You thought it'd be something to see old Billy
shiver in his boots.

Honest, no, Billy.

You're a liar. Learned your trade, gal. Haven't you? I asked ya,
haven't ya?

I couldn't say anything. It's frustrating to have your truths
called lies. I cried and heard Billy whisper shit. He hugged me. I
decided, right then, I'd pay for a few moments in heaven with
hours in hell.

Muguet's silence is like the silence of God. Her silence allows all
other things to be seen and heard. When I met Cass at the Blue
Muzette, all I'd know or hear about was Cass herself. Cass this
and Cass that. Here in my garden of snapdragons with soft,
snapping mouths, and Muguet with her soft, silent mouth, I feel
the sun's heat on my fingers as they slip out of a cool soil-bed. I
forget the poor soil at pa's and the feel of pebbles and shards of
glass on my back when Billy'd snatch at my body and press me
into the ground. Muguet's silence is rapture.

At pa's my dreams were colourful, like they'd been rained on,
like you see in paintings of the Lord. I was chased by a man in
shadow, the devil. Wasn't one hundred per cent he was the devil,
but I felt he was. He offered me wilted tiger lilies and dead pole
bean vines. My hands'd reach out to grab the devil's gifts, and
everything, his hand, the gifts, my hand, turned to dust and the
devil returned to darkness. Nowadays, I feel rested when I wake
up and I can smell the cut grass and soil outside my window and
see the snapdragons, red velvet stigmata against the green of the
crazyhouse hills.

Billy asked me to the county fair. I said yes. I'd a gone to hell and
back with Billy. But only if I came back, for sure. Billy leaned
back against a stranger's car smoking a Winston, I thought,
smelled worse than dog shit, Turkish tobacco.

D'you wanna bring that friend of yours, Cass?

Why? . . . if you want.

I thought you'd like us to be friends. Make it easier for ya.

It's easy enough.

Just thought.

Well, I'll ask – if you think it's a good idea. Whatever.

I had my misgivings. Cass hated Billy. I didn't want a scene, 'specially in front of neighbours who'd gossip, whose words'd filter back to pa's ears. No Ferris wheels or cotton candy had power to ease my mind then. I looked at Billy stabbing at the ground with the tip of his boot, raising little dust-clouds.

I'll ask her.

I regretted those words soon's they fluttered out of my mouth which Billy kissed rough. The rest of my words stuck like chicken bones in my throat.

I asked Cass to come with us to the county fair.

He wanted you to ask me to go?

Yeah.

Why?

I dunno. Wants to be friends, I guess.

Uh-huh. Mind telling me what makes him think I wanna be his friend?

Me.

Well, is it important to ya?

I'd prefer it if you were friends.

All right, I'll go . . . whatcha gonna wear?

Haven't thought it out.

Think I'll wear my hot pink hot pants, them ones my mama got me when she drove to Pensacola year before last.

What you aiming to do with them pants, kill all the old men in town?

That ain't a bad idea, old farts stare at me enough. Serve 'em right.

Cass, why're you always tryin' to outshine me?

What? What you worried about? Billy taking a shine to my bee-hind?

Well, you're wearing somethin' awful provocative to some end.

What're you sayin'? How can you think a thing like that of me?

Can't help it, Cass, something about you inspires that kinda thought. Cass looked at me like I'd slapped her – pale, wide-eyed. Then, as always, I regretted the hurtful words that are the truth.

Next evening, Cass came into the Blue Muzette with a picture of James Dean she'd cut from a magazine. He was walking on a rain-soaked street, shoulders hunched and a cigarette hanging from his lips. She held the picture like it was her own baby. Said she was going to fetch him from Hollywood and bring him home. She was content with her plan till I noted that Dean was dead, body split in half.

What are ya sayin'? You're tryin' to burst my bubble, you sad person.

Cass, it's true. James Dean's been dead a long time. But it's the truth. Ain't my problem you let the truth get to ya.

Just can't let me be happy. It's okay for you to have a beau, pitiful as he is, but I can't even have me a fantasy without you butting in.

Just want you to get the facts straight is all, Cass.

Damn the facts. Fantasy ain't related to facts.

Isn't fantasy when you're aiming to go to Hollywood to fetch back someone who's dead in the ground and split right in two to boot.

You're just a jealous, sad person. Been mistreated all your life so you can't let anyone else enjoy their small share of happiness.

Cass, James Dean is dead. Can't you want someone living?

Yeah, I can. Cass stomped off into the dark, the cornrows in her hair unravelling. She stumbled on a rock and looked back at me. I looked her square in the eye. I didn't mean to bug her, but I was satisfied I had.

Why don't you kiss me more, Billy? It was three months after our first meeting. Early on, I figured things would get better but when they didn't the questions came.

What are you on about, girl?

Just wondering why you hardly kiss me. Other folks kiss lots.

What other folks do ain't my concern.

We were by the riverbank skipping stones and fishing. I was afraid Billy might actually catch something. I didn't want to see a fish hanging off a fishing-rod, dying. Just hanging on, dying.

Concerned with me at all, Billy?

Sure.

Well, I'd like to be kissed.

Asking to be kissed ain't a very attractive quality, girl.

Well, I wish I didn't have to ask. It's a natural thing between a boy and a girl.

Listen, I'll kiss ya if I feel inclined.

I wanted to walk away. But being without Billy meant being with pa so I was strung to Billy. That's why this here crazyhouse is a blessing. As I thought about pa, Billy grabbed me by the shoulders and yanked me to him. He mashed his lips into mine, parted them with his tongue then sucked my tongue into his mouth. Pulled it in. Billy sucked breath out of me. I dizzied and clutched his shoulders to keep standing. When he let go I fell into the dusty bank.

There, you like kissing? Billy spat into the river.

I slid my tongue along my palate to make sure it still worked. But I kept silent. Talk spawns anger. Billy said,

We'll go dancing tonight. Ask Cass to come along.

Billy killed groundhogs for a living. He shot them with his deer-rifle. Sam Foote paid him a dollar a head. Sam Foote worked for some cattle farmers who were sick of losing their cattle to groundhog pits. The cows'd snag themselves in a hole and end up breaking their legs. Beats me why a cow's worthless with a broken leg when a human's worth something even with a broken heart.

There's a fly I've had in my room for a while now. I won't let it out. I watch it zig and zag and buzz towards the window wanting to escape. There's a honey-puddle on the sill which it circles and hovers over. It sits at the puddle's edge, rubbing its forelegs together, then its hindlegs. Its wings, like a filigree of wires, are down close to its body. The sweetness of the honey makes flight unnecessary. I'm waiting for it to drown. There's danger in every attraction, in succumbing. You forget how to fly.

When you first meet up with our county line, and want to cross the line into Melancthon, the first thing you see's a sign telling you not to despair. DON'T DESPAIR in large, black letters. Well, the first thing you do is despair. Each of our hills have little messages poking out of them: TASTE GOD, FEEL GOD, THE BLOOD OF OUR FATHER IS SWEETER THAN SUGAR and the like. Myself, I thought God walked round behind the hills peering at us all. He lived in the water tower that named our town, Atherly. The scariest thing for me was that water tower, imagining God inside readying himself for a day's judgments and pronouncements and hoping I wasn't in his line of vision.

But I was sure his eyes were on pa's house. I hoped God kept track of pa's ways and deeds.

Pa's pa'd been a sailor on the Great Lakes. He'd loaded and unloaded iron ore, grain and steel. All the men on the boats worked long hours, but the money, that never reached their women and children, was good. Port was a sailor's best friend. Whores, liquor and food that stuck to the ribs were a sailor's dream. Granpa, no different than other men, caught the clap and left my pa to make a living on the boats. Liquor was a steady friend to pa from then on. In port and out of port, he kept a steady, ready supply of hootch. Tugs heavy with liquor sidled up to the ships and my pa was the first man overboard. But pa left the boats after a while because he lost his senses to drink. He sent Jim off to the boats but Jim didn't last long. He was none too popular with the other men.

One night, pa stumbled in from a heavy drunk. His liquor smell pluming out of his pores washed over the house. He fumbled his way up the stairs and slammed himself into the railing. I heard his zipper zip and the tinkle of his pee hitting the hallway wall outside my bedroom. Missed the washroom again. I knew the morning was going to be bad so I prayed for a late rise. I got up early, soon as the birds began to twitter and preen outside my window. Pa was shuffling around the kitchen under me. I looked down at him through the hole in the floorboard, small enough to be secret, big enough to see through. Pa was making tap coffee: coffee crystals mixed in hot tap water. His only drink other than liquor. He was grumbling, preparing to cast anger outward at the first one of us to show up in the kitchen. It was hot that day, the backs of my knees and my underarms were wet, my hair all heavy wet strands on my neck. Thankfully, heat dulls pain. I dressed and walked into the hallway past Jim's room. I heard him whisper, sorry, I'm a chicken-shit. Pa heard the stairs creak as I came down them. He stopped his shuffling around. I wasn't scared, it was his custom to wait calmly for prey.

Mornin', pa, I said, when I reached the kitchen. He said nothing, just sipped his coffee. His deer-rifle leaned against the stove. He spoke up after a while,

Who left this here?

At first I didn't know what pa was talking about, then I saw it, a picture of ma, sitting on the counter by the stove. I hadn't left it there and Jim never looked at pictures of ma so I figured pa had left it out.

You lyin' bitch. Which of you? Jim? Pa was coaching me.

Neither of us. Pa threw his coffee cup at the fridge and reached down for his rifle. He brought the end of the barrel up to my nose. Pa was shaking, staring at me. I didn't look away. I prayed he'd shoot me then and there. After a while, he pulled the gun down away from my face and told me to get out. I did, knowing that that wasn't the end of it.

Jim found a dog sitting in the dust on the road to Atherly, dying. Its pain rolled up into its eyes, bones jutted out of its skin which sagged and wrinkled. Jim brought it home and nursed it. He set it up to live in a doghouse built of barnboard. Against pa's will.

Pa won't allow him, I said.

I know. But you can't let a living thing just die.

Things die, Jim.

Long's you're alive you kick against dyin'. You gotta fight.

Pa's gonna kick the life outta ya, Jim.

I'm gonna fight.

Jim kept the dog at first in his room when pa was out drinking. Soon it began to run and play like a normal dog. The fatter it grew the noisier it got. Whimpers, barks then growls. The day came when Jim squared off with pa.

Who's the noisy bastard? Who? Pa'd come back from buying two bottles of hootch from Orville Bullard the county bootlegger. Only place in town that sold liquor on a Sunday was Orville's boast.

What's escaped from the Ark now?

Me, pa, it's me. I got me a dog. I'll take care of him and he's going back outside now, to his doghouse.

He's going back where he come from.

Jim was upstairs sitting on his bed with the dog sitting on his lap. I was in the bathroom. Pa came up the stairs slow and heavy, wheezing from his nose and chest. He went into Jim's room and grabbed the dog by its scruff. It yelped same time as Jim did, No, pa. Please!

Just as I came up to Jim's room, I heard the snapping of bone. Pa broke the dog's neck. It hung like a stuffed toy from his hands. Jim, with his hands covering his face, was crying. I scurried to my room thinking it was too bad the dog had known a few days' peace. Made dying harder. Still, it had had its share of peace. Like the peace in this here crazyhouse.

Church was a part of life for most folks in town although pa never set foot in one. I did, on occasion. Some of the prettier homilies appealed to my ear. The Song of Solomon. The preacher, Benjamin Steers, steered clear of the Bible. He dwelled on the problems that plagued the town.

God did not intend for our cities to be infested with the likes of hammysexuals and sado-masochistical deadbeats. Anyone exhibiting traits of these hyphenated aberrations will experience the wrath of the Almighty . . . While he preached, a single strand of spittle moved between his lips. Droplets of sweat shimmered on his face. The choir slept and the church ladies amened and amened. And after church the ladies nattered about the "hyphenated aberrations" of their neighbours. How Mrs. Percival got married so soon after her husband's death, and how she talked of enjoying sex for the first time in her life. How Mr. Carlson eyed all the young ladies coming into his store to buy jelly beans or jujubes. Far as I could tell, the church ladies didn't see what was really dark in town, what was plain as their own faces, their own nattering.

Cass was reared by her ma, a hairdresser called Lucille who snapped her gum and never got all the hair-dye off her hands. Her biggest customer was her own self. Her hair was blonde and curly, straight and black, brown and short and all combinations in between. She married twice then switched to dating any man who could treat her to steak and nice furnishings. One of her beaux bought her a baby blue Thunderbird which she paid me and Cass a full dollar to clean once a week. She didn't mind me sleeping over, it afforded her the chance to tell me how I could improve myself. I figured I wasn't so bad off since I didn't have a ma who slept with my beaux. Lucille slept with every beau Cass brought home. Lucille was the most popular girl in high school even though she'd never set foot in one. Reverend Steers could've run on and on about Lucille's aberrations.

One night, after I'd been seeing Billy for well on a month, Lucille came up to me through the darkness as I lay on her couch.

You're with the Carstairs boy?

Why, yes . . . ma'm?

Just wonderin'. He's a mighty fine lookin' fella. Somethin' to sink teeth into.

He's nice.

I don't mean anythin' by this but I'm just wonderin' why you think he wants you.

I dunno.

Never mind, honey. Go back to sleeping. Laying in my bed got me to thinking about the boy, is all. And off she clomped into the darkness in baby blue pedal-pushers and pink stilettoes, trailing a smell of sweat and lemon perfume. That night her hair was red.

After a time, Billy and me didn't hold each other, me always arced around his back, like the two of us were spoons. More like flower petals pulling apart at the end of summer. No more sweat between us. The dust siphoned all the moisture from the world, turned it chalky, us into chalk figures. Sometimes our lips met but Billy looked beyond me like there was something waiting for him in the hills outside of town, serried like pa's hunting knife.

Pa's body sprawled on the front porch, and over the tips of his boots he eyed the neighbourhood ladies, and snarled. It was a steady snarling, day in and day out. Kinda funny. The ladies flinched when they caught sight of him, fearful as birds near a tom. Most ladies walked on the opposite side of the road. Pa had no interest in hitching up with no respectable lady or whore. He preferred to drink and frighten anything quieter than his own self. I side-stepped pa's snarling, trying to nudge my way out from under him the way things nudge up from under the soil around here, determined, needing to know what the world above threatens. Like all flowers want the sun and the rain after the sun. So many of them sharing a single small plot and if there is any fightin', there's no show of it, everything living gently, and I still dream of nudging up and out myself, spreading, stretching, living gently.

Or gaily. There were plenty of jamborees and fairs that I attended with Billy. Cass tagged along and jabbed at Billy. He didn't mind, even liked her company. Billy pranced and preened and hugged us both to him whenever other fellas were near. Cass always had a pint of rye whisky with her and we'd all drink from it and end up leaning on each other to get home. One night at a jamboree I lost sight of Billy and Cass. I was by myself a good hour. Funny thing, I felt free. Nothing pressed down. But that passed sure enough. I wanted Billy by my side. Only Cass came back. Billy'd gone home.

Where were you?

Honey, we took a little walk and talked about you practically the whole time.

What'd you say?

Oh, all sorts. Um, how nice you are, too bad about your ma . . .

What'd Billy say?

Said he cares for you.

That all?

What do you want? A speech writ in your honour?

When did you and Billy get so friendly?

I thought I should be nice to your beau, honey.

But you were dead set against him.

I can change my mind, can't I? I gotta go home now, honey.
Cass left, her cornrows thick as bullrushes jostling on her head
and some cherry blossoms clinging to her pink sweater. I wondered how she got them there. Such pretty things.

ELAINE LITTMANN

The Winner's Circle

It was night outside the mall. Jackie had spent the afternoon beneath its cavernous ceilings and bright scrawls of neon. She had taken her daughter to all the toy departments, and fed her fried chicken at the food fair. Now they sat on a plastic bench outside Eaton's. Kaley was squirming beside her, butting her head against Jackie's shoulder. They sat there so long the security guard began to smile at them. He went down the narrow hall to the toilet and came back adjusting his pants, his stare bold and speculative.

Jackie stood up fast, collecting her daughter and her shopping bags. The phone was down the same narrow hall, a slit of grey walls and fluorescent light that hurt her eyes. She called the Winner's Circle, but the bartender said Rainey hadn't shown up yet. When she phoned home there was still no answer, so she hung up. She knew Marlon was there, a silent hump, watching TV in the dark. She had met Rainey in the summer, and moved onto the farm during the broad afternoons and long twilights. The acres of wild grass were so alive with frogs and crickets and wind that sometimes she woke in the brief night and sat up in bed trembling with joy. Winter had brought Marlon, and frozen the fields, and the dark fell so fast it almost hurt. If anything happened now, no-one would hear.

She would have to go to the bar, wait for Rainey and ask him to come home. He wouldn't want to. He managed the band that was playing and he liked to watch them. If she was going to pry him out of there she needed to look good, had to go home and fix her hair, put on her red skirt, and change her shoes, which were hurting her feet. And then there was her daughter. Something had to be done with her for the night, though Kaley wouldn't like that. She was already dragging her feet, tugging angrily away. Even Kaley could tell that home wasn't theirs any more. It wasn't fair, they were there first. Except that wasn't true. Marlon had come first, in every way that mattered, and if Jackie wanted a weapon, it couldn't be that.

The security guard had circled around, he was at the door already, holding it open. "Come back soon." He had a dark, luxurious moustache and excitable eyes. Outside it smelled like snow.

When they reached the farm the house looked empty. But when Jackie climbed out of the van she could see the blue light of the television, flashing off the living room walls like an accident scene. She hoisted Kaley onto her hip and walked across the frozen dirt, looking without much hope for a sign of Rainey. The dogs were loose, restless, and his bike was gone. The front door was locked and there was no point in knocking, so Jackie fished the keys out of her jacket and pushed inside.

Marlon was sitting on the couch, staring at the TV. Jackie stood in the doorway of the living room, waiting for the boy to look up and acknowledge her. She always waited, though she knew by now it wouldn't happen. At first it had given her bitter satisfaction, ammunition for the time when she would tell Rainey he couldn't stay. Tonight, in the scrambled frantic light, it was no longer a game. Marlon frowned, concentrating on the screen, his eyes so deep set he seemed to be pulling them into his skull through sheer force of will. And when Jackie let Kaley slip down onto the floor the little girl stood very still for a moment, looking at Marlon. Then she turned, swift and silent, and put her arms around Jackie's legs. Jackie picked up her daughter and walked back out to the van.

The driveway dipped crossing the drainage pipe and she felt something scrape beneath her. She was driving too fast. The road was a pale spine in the headlights, her leg shook on the accelerator. Rainey could handle Marlon, tell him to turn off the TV, put on the lights, get out from under their feet. Jackie held her breath during these moments, willing Marlon to do something so stubborn and crazy and final that even Rainey couldn't ignore it. But somewhere in whatever thick dreams filled his head, Marlon knew better. So he obeyed, slow as livestock, and Jackie had to turn away to hide from Rainey the look on her face, because she had never wanted to hate his son.

She crossed the bridge to the city lights, heading for her mother's apartment. She wished there was anyone else who could babysit. It exhausted her thinking up excuses, lying about how often she went to the bar. Her mother would never understand how important it was to be with Rainey. She had never met him, and Rainey hadn't made any effort to change that. "She's not going to like me," he said. "Why go through the grief?" So Jackie's mother could let her imagination run wild, thinking the worst. "His past has caught up with him," she would say if she heard about Marlon's arrival. "Next it will be the wife turning up on the doorstep. Well, better now than when it's too late." Too late meant pregnant, again.

Jackie managed to park a block from the building, and Kaley started whining when she realized where they were. Jackie unlocked the seat belt and started lifting Kaley out, but she stiffened her legs. "I don't want to go to Grandma's, I want to go with you."

"Kaley, baby, I'll come pick you up later on, I promise," Jackie said. "You don't want to stay home with Marlon, do you?" That was a mistake. Kaley started to cry, clung to Jackie's neck and grabbed a handful of her hair. Jackie backed out of the van, trying to loosen her child's fist. "Jesus, Kaley, let go. You're hurting me." But if she put Kaley down she'd sit on the sidewalk and howl, and Jackie didn't have time for that. So she hobbled down the icy sidewalk with Kaley twisting her hair and screaming in her ear.

Which was some sight for her mother, opening the door a cautious crack, letting out a wedge of warm stale air and the sound of the TV on too loud. That had been Jackie's first view of her mother for years now, two inches of worried, inquiring face at the door. Her mother kept all the crime clippings from the paper, especially anything to do with missing children. Jackie thought that was at least one thing she'd have in common with Rainey. They could talk about home invasions, and he could come over and install burglar plates and six-inch steel bars on her front door. At least Rainey had a reason, he'd had people trying to kill him. Her mother was just losing her fucking mind.

Kaley got shy all of a sudden, hiding her face against Jackie's jeans.

"Hello, sweetie, it's Grandma. Oh, you were shy like that, when you were that small. Kaley honey, want some of Grandma's cookies?"

"She's tired," Jackie said, keeping her voice steady. "I can put her to bed for you." That might forestall her mother's little investigations. Jackie knew Kaley got put through the third degree, but she couldn't prove it. "Does Grandma ask you lots of questions?" she asked Kaley a while ago. Kaley nodded, but when Jackie said, what does she ask about, the girl's face went vague, evasive. "The name of my dog," she said finally.

Kaley's body had gone slack, exhausted, hopeless. Jackie always felt guilty at this point. The victory was too easy in the end, and too complete, but it didn't feel that way while Kaley was kicking and screaming. Jackie took her to the bathroom, got her into pyjamas and tucked into the little bed. The room was still all white and ruffly, the way her mother had made it up when Jackie was pregnant and living with her. Jackie hadn't the energy to object then, but she'd left everything when she moved out, the chiffon curtains and the bed-ruffle with the hearts on it and the little white dresser with curly gold drawer pulls. She'd had to come back and get the kitten night light because Kaley wouldn't sleep without it.

Jackie came back to the living room. Her feet hurt.

"Do you have something important to do tonight, dear?"

Jackie blinked, tried to keep her face still. "I have to work," she said.

The hotel was called the Furlong, with a pink neon galloping horse. There was a coffee shop and a beer and wine store, and the moving lighted sign said Clarissa Darin and the Outriders in the Winner's Circle. There wasn't a race track nearby, or even a town, it was just an eruption of lights on a fast, dark road. Ranks of Harleys gleamed in the parking lot. A drunk man in a cowboy hat was trying to use the pay phone. Jackie picked her way across the parking lot in the jittery, galloping light.

The bar was hot and dim, a startling blur of noise. The band wasn't on yet. Jackie bought a rye and brandy at the bar. Rainey was at a table near the stage, with Clarissa, and their friend Dave, and Gordie the drummer. Clarissa was leaning so close to Rainey that every time he lifted his glass his arm brushed her breast. She looked up and offered Jackie the kind of dazzled smile she poured over audiences, as if she had stage lights in her eyes.

Rainey saw Jackie coming and gave her his wide, proud drinking grin that still made her heart quicken, made her think everything would be fine. She came around behind him and rubbed his huge shoulders, and he caught her hand and kissed the knuckles. He was thirteen years older than her, and she knew when he was younger she would never have been drawn to him, she would have been too frightened. But now his body had settled, dense and rooted as wood, something she had liked to push against, at first. It made her think of her father's quarter horses, calm and coiled, and almost to be trusted. Their shining, thrusting hindquarters had always made her think about fucking, even when she was too young to know exactly what it meant.

Rainey climbed on the stage to talk to the guitarist, then squatted down to check an amp. It wasn't the kind of bar where the crowd paid attention to the band arriving. Rainey had the brains and the connections to manage some decent acts, and instead he was messing with this outfit whose only outstanding feature was a lead singer with big tits. Jackie wondered if people were talking behind her back.

She watched Rainey, with his long straight hair falling over his face and the engraved silver spur straps glinting on his cowboy boots, in the blue pool of light on the stage. Jackie's mother had gone to bars like this once, the Empress and the Legion back in Roper Lake. After the divorce she said, I only went to keep an eye on your father. God knows what he would have got into if I left him alone. And later, during the years of dire muttering, *pawed by a bunch of drunks*. And now she was muffled alone in her wall-to-wall and her idea of the good life, which was to wipe out every vestige of her old life and not find a thing to replace it with.

Clarissa pulled on her short fringed jacket and went backstage, and the men all stared after her until she disappeared. Then Dave stopped the waitress and ordered Jackie another drink, kissed her on the cheek like an English rock star. He was Rainey's oldest friend and seriously off limits, but she loved the way he looked at her, narrowed and intent, like a dog watching a bird. It was his eyes, so dark the pupils were invisible, and the way he held his face so still that until he laughed or spoke she could never tell what he was thinking.

"How's the evil stepmother?" he asked. He'd known Rainey when they both lived up north with their wives. He'd known Marlon. The one time Jackie had tried to ask about it, Dave said, I don't know, he was just a kid.

Rainey sat down at the table again and stared at the stage, frowning, tapping a rhythm on his thigh with the side of his hand. The stage lights had gone red. Clarissa appeared, and she shone like a candle.

"Honey?" Jackie said.

Rainey turned to look at her, and Jackie could say nothing at all. He just wanted what other people had. The chance to raise his son and make up for all the shit that happened. The way you could, with a normal kid. Rainey might even know already that this wasn't going to happen, but she couldn't say it to him. If she could make Marlon disappear from the face of the earth, even die, she would do it. Then she could carry Rainey through his grief and he would never know she had caused it.

A minute later she was in the washroom, spitting into the sink. She wasn't going to be sick, she'd just had her drinks too fast, she felt dizzy. She spat and spat onto grey paper towels, into the silver teeth of the drain, and then locked herself in a stall and sat on the toilet, put her face in her hands.

She had almost said it. Your son is obscene, he's obsessed. He stares at me all the time, and at Kaley. She'd been trying to say it for weeks. *He doesn't seem to like us very much.* Oh, he's just jealous, Rainey said, he'll get used to you guys. Jackie didn't think Marlon was jealous, because she didn't think he really gave a damn about anything, including his father. The only person he looked at was Kaley. Once Jackie had woken in the dark, some fuzzy frightening dream hour, looked up to see Marlon's round white face in the doorway. Only Rainey's weight beside her kept her from screaming. *He roams around the house at night, I don't want him going in Kaley's room.* But Rainey had insomnia too. "I guess it runs in the family," he said. "I'll talk to him." And he did, finally getting so pissed off at Marlon's sullen silence that he said, "you stay in your room at night or I'll tie you to your goddamn bed." Jackie liked it when he talked like that, but it didn't seem to do any good. And besides, Rainey was gone so often.

It meant so much to him to have his son there finally. He'd made plans for Marlon, Jackie knew, even if he hadn't said much about it. He felt so badly about not being able to see his kids, going on and on about his own childhood and how fucked up it had been, how his ex-wife and her husband treated Marlon like garbage, up there. Worse than garbage, like nothing, made him useless. He didn't even know how to change a light bulb or take out the trash. So what could Jackie say? *Sorry, it's too late. He's only fourteen and he's been destroyed.*

She fixed her makeup and left the bathroom, stopped at the self-serve bar to get another drink. Clarissa was doing "When a Man Loves a Woman," the band limping along behind her trying to make it sound country.

Rainey was smiling, tapping his foot. He looked so happy. Jackie finished her drink and sat holding the glass, watching the dancing couples two-stepping clumsily around the crowded floor. Then she closed her eyes and remembered Rainey playing his fiddle last summer, out on the wide wild lawn, under the moon, his three dogs running dizzy circles on the grass. She'd danced by herself that night, drunk, to that measured, joyful music.

"Are you okay?" It was Dave, touching her arm.

"I should stop drinking," she said. Then, "I have to talk to you."

"We're going to speed it up a bit," Clarissa said in a velvety voice. "You all want to dance, get on up here."

Out in the parking lot Jackie started to shiver. She'd forgotten her jacket.

"Don't worry about Rainey and Clarissa," Dave said. He sounded uneasy. "I mean it. She's nothing to worry about."

"I'm not," Jackie said. She couldn't stop trembling, the night was vast and cold. Traffic swept by on the highway, a lonely track of light and movement, caught in the empty space between places. She felt pity for every person in those cars, and suddenly, achingly, for her daughter, smothering in that lonely white bed. Waking in an unfamiliar room, maybe not forgetting Jackie's promise to come and get her. Maybe Kaley never forgot anything, it just went deep inside her.

"I have to get Kaley," she said. "I shouldn't have left her there."

"Left her where?"

"She's at my mom's."

"Well, she'll be okay there. Come on, Jackie, you can't drive. I'll buy you a coffee."

She felt his hand on her back, all the bones in her spine seemed to twitch. "I want my baby," she said. "I want to go home."

There was a silence. "Look, I'll go get Rainey. He'll take care of you, okay?"

"No," she said. "Not him."

Dave drove her to her mother's apartment, pulled in to the curb and shut off the motor. "Do you want me to go up with you? You going to be okay?"

"No, I'll be fine." She wasn't fine, but she wouldn't be able to explain to her mother who this man was. She unlocked the lobby door, walked up two flights of stairs because she couldn't make herself get in the elevator. The hallway was a dim tunnel, her heels made no sound on the carpet, which felt oddly springy, like walking on mushrooms. She was an invader here, wet, wild-feeling, smelling like the bar and her ears ringing in the stillness, a high faraway sound like long-distance wires. The building throbbed with silence.

It took a long time for her mother to come to the door, peering and clutching her housecoat, the door butting against the chain. "Jackie, good god, do you know what time it is?"

"I've just come to get Kaley."

The door banged. Jackie blinked, thinking, she's finally going to do it. Then the chain scraped and slid, the door swung open again.

"I'm just taking her home, mom, I told you I was going to. It's not that late."

"You can't just go in there and wake her up. And you're not driving in that condition."

"I've got a friend downstairs."

Her mother's lips tightened. Jackie just stood there, marooned on the pale grey carpet, waiting to be released. She'd escaped from her mother twice, the first time when she was eighteen, then again when she'd gone to Rainey. She should have had the sense to stay away, to keep her daughter away. Jackie knew that if her mother said, get to bed, you're disgusting, I know what you do, don't think I'm stupid, she would walk down the hall to the ruffled white room and sit on the floor and cry. The rage and shame seeped out of these walls like a virus. Even Kaley felt it.

Her mother turned her face away. "Well, I suppose I can't stop you," she said.

Jackie went down to the room and knelt by the bed in the dark, touching her daughter awake. "Kaley, honey, we're going to go home now," thinking, please, just don't start crying. Kaley whimpered and blinked, but she didn't cry as Jackie got her dressed, pulling on socks, blue rubber boots, with trembling fingers. One of these days she was simply not going to get out of here, or at least not with Kaley. She was so afraid of losing her that she hadn't tried to put Ricky's name on the birth certificate, had never asked for child support. Sometimes she wondered if she'd had a past life experience. Because she wasn't afraid of her daughter vanishing off the playground, like her mother was, like most mothers were. She was afraid of seeing Kaley pried loose from her, finger by finger, slowly, in plain view, and forever.

Dave said he was going to stop by his house to check on his kids and make her some coffee, and then he'd drive her back to the bar. Jackie held Kaley in her lap and couldn't think of anything to say.

Terry was still up, watching TV. "What's going on?" He was fifteen, and always seemed to be grounded. Jackie didn't even ask why any more.

"Nothing," Dave said. "I'm just on my way back to the bar, I'm going to drop Jackie there and come home. And it's time you got to bed."

"Can I come with you? Just for the ride?" Terry asked, watching his father's face. He was lonely, Jackie recognized it. She saw herself at twelve, thirteen, fourteen, having to come straight home after school, let herself in, watch TV and clean the house until her mother got home from work. She didn't want him around, though, not now.

"All right," Dave said finally. "But leave us alone for a few minutes, okay?" Terry went back to the living room and Dave put coffee on, sat down at the table and looked hard at her. "Rainey's one of my closest friends," he said.

"I know," Jackie said. He thought she was coming on to him. She edged her chair away a bit. "It's just things haven't been so good lately. I wish Marlon hadn't come."

"Yeah, well, I know it's not easy. But you know what it was like for him up there, with his mom and Raider. I mean Raider tried to kill Rainey, and that's not a joke, Jackie. He still would if he ran into him. How do you think it is for Marlon, living with someone who wants his dad dead? You're going to send him back there?"

"I know," Jackie said. He sounded like Rainey, they must have talked about this. "I mean Rainey really admires the way you are with your kids, you know, and so do I, and I guess I thought it would be like that, and it's not. There's something wrong with Marlon, he's not normal. He looks at people so strange."

"He's fourteen, of course he's not normal. Christ, you saw what Terry was like when I got him out of the foster home. I didn't used to want to even leave him alone with his brothers, I really thought he could hurt them. I used to worry about that, Jackie. It just takes some time."

"But Marlon's not like your kids, it's different. Rainey's trying to be a decent guy about this, he's going to get hurt." She leaned across the table, trying to make Dave look at her. "You know how good Rainey is for Terry, he doesn't put up with any shit out of him. And now Terry won't even come around any more."

There was a very long silence. "You're saying just throw Marlon away?"

"He was always really weird." That was Terry, in the doorway.

Dave looked over, fast. "I told you to stay out of here."

"I just wanted to get a Coke," Terry said. He sounded scared.

"What do you mean?" Jackie said, but Terry backed out and disappeared. She turned to Dave. "What did he mean?"

"I don't know. Kid stuff. There was nothing wrong with Marlon that I ever saw." He still wasn't looking at her. "Come on, Jackie, you've got a kid. What if it was Kaley in that situation, wouldn't you want someone to help her out?"

But Jackie thought if her daughter ever looked at her with those vacant eyes she would shrivel up inside. She'd know something had been done to Kaley that would never be made right.

After that little scene, she didn't think Terry would come with them, but he followed them out to the truck, tentatively, as if he expected his father to tell him to get back inside. Dave jammed a blues tape into the stereo and turned it up, too loud to talk unless you really needed to. Terry was nodding his head to the music, probably just happy to be out of the house. Jackie couldn't believe Dave could look at her so closely sometimes, as if he was drawing the thoughts right out of her skull, and not hear her now. Not want to help her.

"I'll wait here," she said when they pulled into the parking lot. "I can't take Kaley in." She could hear the band grinding away behind the walls of the hotel. The neon horse galloped over their heads, shedding pink light along the dashboard of the truck, running nowhere. She waited until Dave disappeared into the bar and then said, "Terry, listen, what were you saying back there?"

"What?" he said. "Nothing."

"Look, please tell me, okay? I won't say anything to Rainey, I won't tell your dad."

Terry looked up at the neon horse for a minute. He reminded Jackie of Kaley, when she tried to get an answer out of her. Finally he said, "Well, I don't know, it's just he was weird. He wet the bed all the time."

"What else? What sort of things did he do?" She wanted tortured cats or something, evidence.

"We just didn't like him, he always tried to hang around with us, we'd have to ditch him. And we didn't like going over to his house, his mom was always whaling on him, she was a maniac. And we could never make any noise because Rainey was sleeping."

"Was he violent?"

Terry gave her an uneasy, slanting look, shrugged. "Well, sometimes, I guess. I mean, me and my brothers stayed there a lot when my parents were out of town, and he never hit me or nothing, or not much anyway. Not hard. Marlon got it a lot, I guess. But he kind of deserved it."

"What?" Jackie said.

"We don't talk about Elliot River much."

The door of the truck opened and Rainey was standing there, one arm slung along the top of the window, smiling at her.

"Jackie, Jackie, Jackie," he said, shaking his head. "What the hell are you doing?"

She felt Terry grow very still beside her.

"Nothing," she said.

Rainey loaded his bike in the van and drove them home, talking about Clarissa, how someone had offered her a recording deal. He was half drunk, and she knew she should put Kaley in the car seat, but she didn't want to let go of her. Anyway, there were no other cars on the road. They were soaring through a blackness so dense they could be flying, the lights of the van picking up the occasional mail box, the shallow yawn of farm drive. About halfway up Pit Road Rainey said, "You knew I had a family when we got together."

"I know," Jackie said.

"You don't know."

Jackie looked out the window, because there was no answer for that. What had happened in the past, what he thought he owed his son, she didn't know. She only knew that when he failed with Marlon, she and Kaley might not survive. Not as his family.

When they got home, Marlon was asleep on the couch, the TV finally silent. At least he had tidied the living room a bit, put away his comics and baseball cards. Jackie had been surprised at first by his toys and models, she thought he was past that age. One day she saw him playing with a toy car, running it along the back of the couch and down the arm, along the seam of his jeans, his face absorbed and dreamy. Rainey said his ex-wife once found Marlon sniffing gas in the basement.

Jackie put Kaley to bed, not bothering to undress her, just pulling off her boots and jacket, kissing her hot damp hair. She spent a long time in the bathroom, but when she came to the bedroom Rainey was still sitting on the edge of the bed, naked, in the dark. She lay down and pulled the blankets over her, felt the mattress sink as he crawled in. She hoped he didn't want to make love, it hadn't been good lately, and it wouldn't be tonight. She still loved how massive he was, though at first his weight had been frightening, like a bear rolling on top of her. When he went too deep, she ached inside, a cramping twinge that took her breath away. The first time it happened she felt crazy, like he was reaching a place that should never be touched. She'd had to tell him, and after that he held back. But when he was angry, he didn't.

He didn't turn to her, tonight. He said, "I saw in the paper today, another place in Ontario."

Jackie closed her eyes. She used to want to hear Rainey talk about his childhood, about the places he'd had to live. She used to think it meant something.

"I could find that guy," he said. "He wasn't that old. I bet he's still out there, I bet he's still working with kids. I mean, they've got to have records. They've got to have his last name."

"Rainey, please," she said.

"If they can hunt Nazis down after fifty years, I can find this guy. I don't give a shit if he's eighty years old. And you know what, maybe I wouldn't even bother with the cops and everything, I mean who the fuck knows if they'd do anything. Maybe they couldn't find anyone else who was there."

"I know," she said. "I know."

"Maybe I'll just handle it myself. I've thought about that for a long time."

"I know."

He rolled over and trapped her legs with his, moved on top of her. She didn't try to stop him. He pushed himself up on his elbows, held his weight off her, his cock lying hard and hot against her belly, making her tremble. She didn't want to open her legs, she didn't want to move. He kissed her mouth, her throat, her breasts. She felt his long hair brush her body, which at first had seemed so strange, like making love with another girl. And she stroked his hot, fierce, dry skin, the wide rise of his back, because she knew he would do it anyway, in the end.

He pushed her hair off her face and looked at her in the dark. She couldn't see his eyes but it didn't matter, she could never read them.

"Ready?" he said.

"Yes."

He tightened his fingers in her hair so hard she almost whimpered, and pushed inside. It didn't hurt. It was what he wanted, and it didn't hurt. He pounded in her for a long time, he couldn't come, he tangled her hair and battered against her until she was crying, tight and silent. Not in pain, but with a loneliness so wide and absolute that it seemed to be the end of any road she could have taken. The deepest point of love contained no sanctuary, only a wall that would never be breached, beyond it a wilderness.

In the morning Marlon came and sat at the kitchen table.

"Where is he?" He never called Rainey Dad.

"In bed, where else," Jackie said. Rainey was never up before ten. "Kaley, honey, you're finished. Go watch TV." Kaley gave Marlon a sideways look, then squirmed in her chair and licked her fingers.

"I cleaned up," Marlon said. "Like you said."

Jackie scraped fried eggs out of the pan and set the plate down in front of him so hard the yolks broke. No-one could say she didn't look after him. She felt the same way when she watched Rainey's Malamutes eat. And the living room rug was still gritty with crumbs, the sink full of dirty dishes.

Marlon shifted his shoulders a bit, like he was embarrassed. "I cleaned up," he said again. Then he hunched over his plate and picked up his fork. Jackie looked away, she couldn't stand watching him chew with his mouth open. This was new, his attempt to please her, but he probably sensed something was up.

Jackie left him eating and went into the living room. She had to call twice before Kaley finally slid off the chair and followed, with one last curious look at Marlon. Jackie handed her daughter the channel changer to play with, though the static and tumble through chipmunk cartoons and Sunday preachers gave her a headache. She tugged the musky-smelling blankets off the couch and turned over the cushions. A red model car tipped off the arm of the couch and landed upside down on the rug, its wheels spinning. Kaley picked it up.

"Don't touch that, sweetie, it's Marlon's."

Kaley kept her head down, rolling the wheels back and forth with the flat of her hand.

"She can play with it if she wants." He was standing in the doorway. "I don't play with them any more." Then he walked towards the TV and squatted beside Kaley, touched the car with his thick soft fingers. Jackie could still smell his blankets, was sure the odour of him was on her hands.

"She has her own toys," she said. She couldn't see Marlon's face, only his big slumped shoulders, the slab of his waist, the fat, creased wrists, like a baby's. "She's too young to play with you," she said. "Don't play with her. Just don't."

Rainey got up around eleven and said he was going to drive the dogs up to the old gravel pits before lunch. Marlon was on the couch watching TV, eating dry cereal out of a box. They could hear the gulping chatter of cartoons, *golly, Speed Racer, what are we gonna do now*.

"Maybe he wants to come," Rainey said.

Jackie slid plates into the sink. Some mornings Rainey seemed to fill the kitchen until she had trouble breathing. "I wish he'd help out once in a while."

"So tell him."

"You know he doesn't listen to me."

"Yeah, so I hear." He was leaning in the doorway, arms folded, staring at her. Jackie felt the pulse behind her ear quicken. Dave had talked.

"Take him for a walk, then," she said. "I don't care."

Rainey turned to the living room. "Hey, Marlon, you ever going to get your ass off that couch? Come on, come get some exercise." And he slapped his thigh twice, the way he called his dogs.

Marlon said something that Jackie couldn't hear. Rainey must not have, either, because he took a few steps into the living room and said, "Pardon me?"

"I said I don't feel too good."

Jackie turned back to the sink and cranked the hot water tap. She did not want to be a witness. A moment later she felt Rainey cross the kitchen. He didn't even touch her as he passed behind her back, but still she moved away, washed up against the counter in his wake. The door banged. And then the TV, suddenly so loud she could hear it above the water steaming into the sink.

Rainey was back in an hour, icy air clinging to his clothes. The Malamutes lay under the table, panting. Jackie made ham sandwiches and soup, a can of spaghetti for Kaley, unwrapped a cherry pie.

"I'm going out to my brother's this afternoon, he's got a couple of parts for the van," Rainey said. He seemed in a better mood. "You all want to come, we can make a day of it."

"Oh, a car day, why not," Jackie said. She leaned over his back to pour coffee, let her breasts rest on his shoulder for a moment. He reached for the milk. At the edge of her vision she saw Marlon glance up.

"Well, the other thing," Rainey said, "is Dave's going to be up there, he wants to buy that old Falcon for Terry. I told them I'd check it over."

"Are you serious?" Jackie said. "He's only fifteen."

"Yeah, well." Rainey glanced over at Marlon, head down over his pie plate. "Hey, get your elbows off the table. Kaley eats better than you do." He grinned and nudged him. Marlon drew his elbows in to his sides and straightened his back, began eating faster. "He thinks it'll give him something to do, keep him off the street. I told him don't do it. You give a kid a car he's not allowed to drive yet, you're asking for trouble. He says he won't give him the keys. I said, yeah, that's going to stop Terry for about half a minute. Not to mention his friends."

"Oh, well. I guess he's got to start trusting him sometime," Jackie said, but she was watching Marlon reach for a third piece of pie. He'd eat the whole thing if she didn't put it away.

"Oh, bullshit," Rainey said. "That's not what it's about. Terry wants it, Terry gets it. Dave just spoils him rotten, always has. Isn't that right, you remember that?" He reached over and rapped Marlon on the shoulder with the back of his knuckles. Marlon blinked, raised his head like someone searching for a sound in the dark.

"You going to come with us, or have you got something of national importance to watch on the TV, there?" Rainey said.

Marlon bent his head again and shovelled a forkful of pie into his mouth, then another, too fast to chew.

"Marlon?" Rainey said. His voice had gone cautious.

Marlon's jaw worked frantically, cherry juice dribbled down his chin. Jackie saw something in his eyes that looked like panic.

"Honey," she said, very carefully, touching Rainey on the arm. "Maybe just leave him alone."

Marlon's pie was gone. His plate was a bloody scrape of red.

Rainey drove, fast and silent. They didn't even say goodbye to Marlon, back on the couch with his rock videos. Jackie watched the road, the new subdivisions that had sprouted out of the frozen, ploughed-over fields. They looked raw and stranded and wavery somehow, as if she was seeing them through an icy window.

Finally Rainey cleared his throat. "You know," he said. "Maybe you're right, there. He doesn't seem to be settling in too good."

"He probably misses his friends and stuff." She could be more generous now, the dance had begun. "Maybe he's homesick."

"I don't think Marlon has any friends, to tell you the truth."

There was another silence. Jackie stroked the fringe on her scarf and felt a hard bit of grief in her throat. Rainey had wanted his son back and instead he got a zombie. Jackie could feel the love that both of them had been summoning up, preparing for Marlon's arrival. It swirled around them in the cold, rattling van, it had become something else. Jackie knew she could stop this, say *let's try to help him*. If she really loved Rainey, if she was truly a giving person, she should have the strength. But she didn't. Rainey didn't deserve this, she and Kaley didn't deserve it. *Don't try*, she wanted to say. *Don't even try*.

Dave bought the car, and then they all went for supper at the Bamboo Garden on the Grover Road exit. They stayed drinking wine until the karaoke started, then drove back to Dave's to drink beer and play music. Jackie rocked Kaley in her lap and sang along in her ear, imagined her grown up and singing with a band, shining and beautiful under the lights.

On the way home Rainey was quiet again.

"What are you thinking about?" Jackie asked finally. She wanted to finish this tonight.

Rainey shrugged, squinting against a passing car. "Turn your fucking high beams off," he said, then, "I don't know. That maybe it's not working out."

For a second she thought he meant them, her. Then she said, carefully, watching the side of his face, "He doesn't seem to feel anything. It's like he doesn't care."

"Yeah, well, he's been through a lot."

"Were you like that, then, when you were his age? You went through a lot worse than Marlon has."

There was a silence. "I didn't treat him too good," Rainey said. His voice was so low it wove into the sound of the engine, the road droning under them.

She closed her eyes for a minute, gathering strength. "He is not your fault, Rainey, you haven't even seen him in four years. You're always telling me to quit feeling guilty about things."

"I don't feel guilty."

She waited for more, but it didn't come. "Rainey, please. He scares me. I mean, if he'd let us know, just once, how he feels about something, it would be different. He's not happy, he's not mad, nothing. He's like a zero." And then she remembered she was talking about his child. "He doesn't even like you," she said. But she said it so quiet she wasn't sure he heard.

When they got home the house was dark, though it wasn't that late. Marlon's shape was humped on the couch. Jackie went down to the bathroom and switched on the light, saw the red, cherry-pie vomit in the toilet. She flushed it and turned the light out again, went into the bedroom where Rainey was sitting on the bed pulling his boots off.

"You tired?" she said, and climbed onto the wide bed, worked her way across it on her knees and slid her arms around his shoulders. He dropped a boot on the floor and unbuckled his belt. "Honey?" she said, and lifted his hair, kissed the back of his neck. She didn't like the feeling in his body, but if there was one night he should be able to take it out on her, this would be it. She'd welcome it, it would be her penance.

Rainey twisted his neck away, stood up. "I'm going to take a bath," he said, and walked out. Jackie sat in the middle of the bed until she knew she wasn't going to cry, and then she got up and followed him. She could hear the taps running, but he had the door pulled almost shut.

"Kaley?" she said, lifting her head. She wasn't in her room. Jackie breathed very carefully, feeling her heart begin to pound. She couldn't hear anything but the hiss of the plumbing. "Kaley?" So soft, almost a whisper. She moved down the hall to the living room, holding her breath. If this was it, there would be no question now.

Kaley was standing alone, in the centre of the room. She turned her head as Jackie came to the doorway, her eyes wide, but not frightened.

"Marlon's sad," she said.

Marlon was crying, maybe in his sleep. But Jackie thought he was awake, for the sound was so dry and shrunken, pulled out of his throat like stitches. He was rolled in his blankets, she couldn't see his face. It was like listening to someone die, some- one she didn't know and couldn't reach.

She picked up Kaley and carried her down the hall. The crack of the bathroom door let out a stripe of light and the sound of water roaring into the tub, a faint, high whine deep in the pipes. Very quietly, Jackie pulled the door closed, felt the tongue of the lock slide into the frame.

She put Kaley to bed. Then she went into the kitchen and got a yellow candle, lit it and went to the bathroom. She switched off the overhead light and set the candle on the counter. The bathtub was a big clawfooted one, but Rainey sat in it with his knees up, hunched over like a child. She blinked, trying to see him better in the steam and the candle light. He didn't look up. She held her breath for a moment, listening, but all she could hear was the small swallowing sound of the tap dripping.

She sat down in the chair she used to bathe Kaley, and rolled up her sleeves. She gathered Rainey's hair behind his neck. The ends were wet. She began to braid it, her fingers trembling.

He said something, too low to hear. Jackie leaned across his shoulders, hardly breathing.

"I should go talk to him," Rainey said.

"No," Jackie said. "He's asleep." She stroked the back of his neck. "He ate the rest of the pie, I knew he would. Now he's just asleep."

She picked up the wash cloth and wrung it out across his back, sheening his skin and making it gleam, like wetting a stone. Then she began to wash his back in long, slow strokes, feeling how his muscles had begun to slip a bit loose from the bones, from the hard bows of his ribs, like the coats of his dogs, loose for fighting. Her fingers moved carefully, searching for a crack in the cliff of his body, a shifting of the ancient earth that could lift her to safety.

ELIZABETH HAY

The Friend

She was thirty, a pale beautiful woman with long blonde hair and high cheekbones, small eyes, sensuous mouth, an air of serenity and loftiness – superiority – and under that, nervousness, insecurity, disappointment. She was tired. There was the young child who woke several times a night. There was Danny who painted till two in the morning then slid in beside her and coaxed her awake. There was her own passivity. She was always willing even though she had to get up early, and always resentful, but never resentful out loud. She complied. In conversation she was direct and Danny often took part in these conversations, but in bed, apparently, she said nothing. She felt him slide against her, felt his hand between her legs, its motion the reverse of a woman wiping herself, back to front instead of front to back. She smelled paint – the air of the poorly ventilated attic where he worked – and felt his energetic weariness and responded with a weary energy of her own.

He didn't speak. He didn't call her by any name (during the day he called her Moe more often than Maureen). He reached across her and with practised efficiency found the Vaseline in the bedside drawer.

I met her one afternoon on the sidewalk outside the neighbourhood grocery store. It was sunny and it must have been warm – a Saturday in early June. Our section of New York was poor and Italian, and we looked very different from the dark women around us. The friendship began with that shorthand – shortcut to each other – an understanding that goes without saying. I had a small child too.

A week later, at her invitation, I walked the three blocks to her house and knocked on the front door. She opened a side door and called my name. "Beth," she said, "this way." She was dressed in a loose and colourful quilted top and linen pants. She looked composed and bohemian and from another class.

Inside there was very little furniture: a sofa, a chest, a rug, Danny's paintings on the wall. He was there. A small man with Fred Astaire's face and an ingratiating smile. Once he started to talk, she splashed into the conversation. She commented on everything he said, changing it and making it convoluted out of what I supposed was a desire to be included. Only later did I realize how much she insisted on being the centre of attention, and how successfully she became the centre of mine.

We used to take our kids to the only playground within walking distance. It was part of a school yard, and marked the border between our neighbourhood and the next. The pavement shimmered with broken glass, the kids were wild and unattended. We pushed our two on the swings and kept each other company. She said she would be so mad if Danny got AIDS, and I thought about her choice of words – "so mad" – struck by the understatement.

I learned about sex from her the way girls learn about sex from each other. In this case the information came not in whispered conversations behind a hedge but more directly and personally than anything I might have imagined at the age of twelve.

In those days the hedge was high and green, and the soil below it dark – a setting that was at once private and natural and fenced off.

This time everything was in the open. I was the audience, the friend with stroller, a mild-mannered wide-eyed listener who learned that breastfeeding brought Maureen to the point of orgasm, that childbirth had made her vagina sloppy and loose, that anal sex hurt so much she would sit on the toilet afterwards and brace herself against the stabs of pain.

We were in the playground (that sour, overused, wrongly used, hardly playful patch of pavement) and she said she was sore and told me why. When I protested on her behalf she said, "But I might have wanted it. I don't know. I think I did want it in some way."

I can't remember her hands, not here in this small cool room in another country and several years after the fact. I remember watching her do many things with her hands; yet I can't remember what they look like. They must be long, slender, pale unless tanned. But they don't come to mind the way a man's might and I suppose that's because she didn't touch me. Or is it because I became so adept at keeping her at bay? I remember her lips, those dry thin Rock Hudson lips.

One evening we stood on the corner and she smiled her fleeting meaningful smiles and looked at me with what she called her northern eyes (they were blue and she cried easily) while her heartbreak of a husband put his arm around her. What will become of her, I wondered, even after I found out.

She was standing next to the stove and I saw her go up in flames: the open gas jets, the tininess of the room, the proximity of the children – standing on chairs by the stove – and her hair. It slid down her front and fell down her back. She was making pancakes and they were obviously raw. She knew they were raw, predicted they would be, yet did nothing about it. Nor did I. I just poured on lots of syrup and said they were good.

I saw her go up in flames, or did I wish it?

In the beginning we saw each other almost every day and couldn't believe how much the friendship had improved our lives. A close, easy, intensity which lasted in that phase of its life for several months. My husband talked of moving – an apartment had come open in a building where we had friends – and I couldn't imagine moving away from Maureen.

It was a throwback to girlhood – the sort of miracle that occurs when you find a friend with whom you can talk about everything.

Maureen had grown up rich and poor. Her family was poor, but she was gifted and received scholarships to private schools.

It was the private school look she'd fixed on me the first time we met, and the poor background she offered later. As a child she received nothing but praise, she said, from parents astonished by their good fortune: They had produced a beautiful and brilliant daughter in a larger context of everything going wrong: accidents, sudden deaths, mental illness.

Danny's private school adjoined hers. They met when they were twelve and he never tried to hide his various obsessions. She could never say that she had never known.

In the spring her mother came to visit. The street was torn up for repairs, the weather prematurely hot, the air thick with dust. Maureen had spread a green cloth over the table and set a vase of cherry blossoms in the middle. I remember the shade of green and the lushness of the blossoms because everything about Maureen was usually scattered and in disarray.

Her mother was tall and more attractive in photographs than in person. In photographs she was still, in person she darted about, and there was something high-pitched and unrelenting about the way she moved. When she spoke she left the same impression – startling in her abnormality and yet apparently normal. She spoke in a rapid murmur as though after years of endless talking about the same thing she now made the sounds that people heard: they had stopped up their ears long ago.

She talked about Maureen. How precocious she had been as a child, reading by the age of four, and by the age of five memorizing whole books.

"I remember her reading a page, and I told her to go and read it to Daddy. And she said, 'with or without the paper?' Lots of children can read at five, even her brother was reading at five, but few have Maureen's stamina. She could read for hours, and adult books. I had to put Taylor Caldwell on the top shelf."

A photograph of the child was tacked to the wall in Danny's studio. She was seated in a chair and wearing one of those very short summer dresses we used to wear that ended well above bare round knees. Her face was unforgettable. It was more than beautiful. It had a direct, knowing, almost luminous look produced by astonishingly clear eyes and fair, fair skin. Already she knew enough not to smile.

"That's her," said Danny. "There she is."

The beautiful kernel of the beautiful woman.

She had always imagined bodies firmer than hers, but not substantially different. She had always imagined Danny with a boy.

I met the lover without realizing it. It was June again, and we were at their house in the country. A shaded house beside a stream – cool, green, quiet – the physical manifestation of the serenity I once thought she possessed. A phrase in a movie review: her wealth so old it had a patina. Maureen's tension so polished it had a veneer.

All weekend I picked her long hairs off my daughter's sweater and off my own. I picked them off the sheet on the bed. I picked blackberries and they left hair-like scratches on my hands.

My hands felt like hers. I looked down at my stained fingers and they seemed longer. I felt the places where her hands had been: changing diapers, buttoning shirts, deep in tofu and tahini, closing in on frogs which she caught with gusto. Swimming, no matter how cold.

I washed my hands and lost that feeling of being in contact with many things. Yet the landscape continued – the scratches if not the smells, the sight of her hands and hair.

An old painter came to visit. He parked his station wagon next to the house and followed Danny into his studio in the barn. Maureen and I went off with the kids to pick berries.

The day was hot and humid. There would be rain in the night and again in the morning. We followed a path through the woods and came to a stream. The kids splashed around, Maureen and I hung our legs over the bank. Her feet were long and slender, mine were wide and short. We sent ripples of water towards the kids.

She told me that Henry – the painter's name was Henry – was Danny's mentor, they had known each other for years and he was a terrible alcoholic. Then she leaned close and her shoulder touched mine. One night last summer Danny had come back from Henry's studio and confessed – confided – that he had let the old man blow him off. Can you believe it? And she laughed. Giddy – flushed – breathless – excited. A warm breeze blew a strand of her hair into my face. I brushed it away and it came back – ticklish, intimate, warm and animal-like. I didn't find it unpleasant, not at the time.

We brought the berries back to the house, and late in the afternoon the two men emerged and sat with us on the veranda. Henry was whiskery, gallant, shy. Maureen talked a great deal and laughed even more. Before dark, Henry drove away.

She knew. It all came out the next spring and she pretended to be horrified, but she knew.

That night sounds woke me: Danny's low murmur, Maureen's uninhibited cries. I listened for a long time. It must have occurred to me then that the more gay he was, the more she was aroused.

~

I thought it was someone come to visit. But the second time I realized it was ice falling. At midday, icicles fall from the eave-strough into the deep snow below.

And the floor which I keep sweeping for crumbs? There are no crumbs. The sound comes from the old linoleum itself. It crackles in the cold.

Often I wake at one or two in the morning, overheated from the hot water bottle, the three blankets, the open sleeping bag spread on top. In my dreams I am taking an exam over and over again.

In the morning I go down in the socks I've worn all night to turn up the heat and raise the thin bamboo blind through which everyone can see us anyway. I make coffee, then scald milk in a hand-beaten copper pot with a long handle. In Quebec there is an expression for beating up egg whites: *monter en neige*. Milk foams up and snow rises.

Under the old linoleum old newspapers advertise an "equipped one bedroom at Lorne near Albert" for $175. Beside the porch door the linoleum has broken away, and you can read mildew, dust, grit, *Ottawa Citizen*, 1979. The floor is a pattern of squares inset with triangles and curlicues in wheat shades of immature to ripe. Upstairs the colours are similar but faded; and flowers, petals.

During the eclipse I saw Maureen when I saw the moon. I saw my thumb inch across her pale white face.

I have no regrets about this. But I have many thoughts.

We pushed swings in the playground while late afternoon light licked at the broken glass on the pavement. New York's dangers were all around us, and so was Maureen's fake laugh. She pushed William high in the swing, and when he came back she let out a little trill.

It was the time of Hedda Nussbaum. We cut out the stories in the newspaper and passed them back and forth – photographs of Hedda's beaten face, robust husband, abused and dead daughter. It had been going on for so long. Hedda had been beaten for thirteen years, the child was seven years old.

In the playground, light licked at the broken glass and then the light died and we headed home, sometimes stopping first for tea at her house. Her house always had a loose and welcoming atmosphere which hid the sharp edge of need against which I rubbed.

She began to call before breakfast. She dressed me with her voice, her worries, her anger, her malleability. Usually she was angry with Danny for staying up so late that he was useless all day, of no help in looking after William, while she continued to work to support them, to look after the little boy in the morning and evening, to have no time for herself. But when I expressed anger on her behalf she defended him . . .

Similarly with the stomach pains. An ulcer, she suggested, then made light of the possibility when I took it seriously.

She often asked, "Is this all? Is this going to be my contribution?" She was referring to her brilliant past and her sorry present. She didn't like her job, didn't like the neighbourhood, kept talking about the men she could have married. Motherhood gave her something to excel at. She did everything for her son – dressed him, fed him, directed every moment of play. "Is this all right, sweetie? Is this? What about this? Then, sweetie pie, what do you want?"

Sweetie pie wanted what he got. His mother all to himself for a passionately abusive hour, then peace, affection. During his tantrums she embraced him and tried to distract him, the two of them behind a closed door. She would emerge and smile and shake her head. "That was short. You should see what they're like sometimes."

Even when Danny offered to look after him, even when he urged her to take a long walk, she refused. Walked, but briefly, back and forth on the same sidewalk, or up and down the same driveway. Then she returned out of a sense of responsibility to the child. But the child was fine.

At two years he still nursed four or five times a night, and her nipples were covered with scabs. "But the skin there heals so quickly," she said.

We moved to the other side of the city and the full force of it hit me. I remember bending down under the sink of our new apartment, still swallowing a mouthful of peanut butter, to cram S.O.S pads into the hole – against the mouse, taste of it, peanut butter in the trap. Feel of it, dry and coarse under my fingers. Look of it, out of the corner of my eye a small dark slipper. Her hair always in her face, and the way I was ratting on her.

It got to the point where I knew the phone was going to ring before it rang. Instead of answering, I stood there counting. Thirty rings. Forty. Once I said to her, I think you called earlier, I was in the bathroom and the phone rang forever. Oh, she said, I'm sorry, I wasn't even paying attention. Then I saw the two of us: Maureen mesmerized by the act of picking up a phone and holding it for a time; and me, frantic with resentment about which I did nothing.

"Why is she so exhausting?" I asked my husband, then answered my own question. "She never stops talking and she always talks about the same thing."

But I wasn't satisfied with my answer. "She doesn't want solutions to her problems. That's what's so exhausting."

And yet that old wish – a real wish – to get along. I went to bed thinking about her, woke up thinking about her and something different yet related. The two mixed together in a single emotion. I had taken my daughter to play with a friend: Another girl was already there and they didn't want Annie to join them. I woke up thinking of my daughter's rejection, my own various rejections, and Maureen.

It seemed inevitable that he would leave her – clear that he was gay and inevitable that he would leave her. He was an artist. To further his art he would pursue his sexuality. But I was wrong. He didn't leave her, and nor did I.

Every six months he had another gay attack and talked, thought, drew penises. Every six months she reacted predictably and never tired of her reactions. Her persistence took on huge, saintly proportions.

I never initiated a visit or a call, but I didn't make a break. As yielding as she was – and she seemed to be all give – I was even more so, apparently.

Tensions accumulated – the panic as she continued to call and I continued to come when called, though each visit became more abrasive, more insulting, as though staged to show who cared least: You haven't called me, you never call me, you think you can make up for your inattention with this visit but I'll show you that I don't care either: the only reason I'm here is so that my son can play with your daughter.

We walked along the river near her country place. William was on the good tricycle, my daughter was on the one that didn't work. Maureen said, "I don't think children should be forced to share. Do you? I think kids should share when they want to share."

Her son wouldn't give my daughter a turn the whole long two-hour walk beside the river – with me pointing out what? Honeysuckle. Yes, honeysuckle. Swathes of it among the rocks. And fishermen with strings of perch. I stared out over the river, unable to look at Maureen and not arguing; I couldn't find the words.

With each visit there was the memory of an earlier intimacy, and no interest in resurrecting it.

Better than nothing. Better than too much. And so it continued, until it spun lower.

The visit to the country marked my swing from blind acceptance to blind criticism, the natural conclusion of an unnaturally warm friendship. We were sitting on the mattress in Danny's studio in front of a wall-size mirror. Around us were his small successful paintings and his huge failures. He insisted on painting big, she said, because he was so small. "I really think so. It's just machismo."

How clear-eyed she was.

I rested my back against the mirror, Maureen faced it. She glanced at me, then the mirror, and each time she looked in the mirror she smiled slightly. Her son was there. He wandered off, and then it became clear that she was watching herself.

She told me she was pregnant again. It took two years to persuade Danny, "and now he's even more eager than I am," and she smiled at herself.

Danny got sick. I suppose he'd been sick for months, but I heard about it the next spring. Maureen called in tears. "The shoe has dropped," she said.

He was so sick that he had confessed to the doctors that he and Henry – old dissipated Henry whose cock had slipped into who knows what – had been screwing for the last five years. Maureen talked and wept for thirty minutes before I realized that she had no intention of leaving him, or he of leaving her. They would go on. The only change, and this wasn't certain, was that they wouldn't sleep together. They would go to their country place in June and stay all summer.

I felt cheated, set up, used. "Look, you should do something," I said. "Make some change."

She said, "I know. But I don't want to precipitate anything. Now isn't the time."

She said it wasn't AIDS.

Her lips dried out like tangerine sections separated in the morning and left out all day. She nursed her children so long that her breasts turned into small apricots, and now I cannot hold an apricot in my hand and feel its soft loose skin, its soft nonweight, without thinking of small spent breasts – little dugs.

She caught hold of me, a silk scarf against an uneven wall, and clung.

Two years later I snuck away. In the weeks leading up to the move, I thought I might write to her afterwards, but in the days right before, I knew I would not. One night in late August when the weather was cool and the evenings still long, we finished packing at nine and pulled away in the dark.

We turned right on Broadway and rode the traffic in dark slow motion out of the city, north along the Hudson, and home.

In Canada I thought about old friends who were new friends because I hadn't seen them for such a long time. And newer friends who were old friends because I'd left them behind in the other place. I noticed I had no landscape in which to set them. They were portraits in my mind (not satisfying portraits either because I couldn't remember parts of their bodies; their hands, for instance, wouldn't come to mind). They were emotion and episode divorced from time and place. Yet there was a time – the recent past, and a place – a big city across the border.

And here was I, where I had wanted to be for as long as I had been away from it – home – and it didn't register either. In other words, I discovered that I wasn't in a place. I was the place. I felt populated by old friends. They lived in my head amid my various broodings. Here they met again and went through the same motions and different ones. Here they coupled in ways that hadn't occurred really. And here was I, disloyal but faithful, occupied by people I didn't want to see and didn't want to lose.

August came and went, September came and went, winter didn't come. It rained in November and it rained in December. In January a little snow fell, then more rain.

Winter came when I was asleep. One morning I looked out at frozen puddles and a small dusting of snow. It was very cold. I stepped carefully into the street and this is what I saw. I saw the landscape of friendship. I saw Sunday at four in the afternoon. I saw childhood panic. People looked familiar to me, yet they didn't say hello. I saw two people I hadn't seen in fifteen years – one was seated in a restaurant, the other skated by. I looked at them keenly and waited for recognition to burst upon them, but it didn't.

On the other hand, strangers claimed to recognize me. They said they had seen me before, some said precisely where. "It was at a conference two years ago." Or, "I saw you walk by every day with your husband last summer. You were walking quickly."

But last summer I had been somewhere else.

The connections were wistful, intangible, maddening. Memory tantalized and finally failed. Yet as much as memory failed, those odd unhinged conjunctures helped. Strange glimmerings and intense looks were better than nothing.

The last time I saw Maureen, she was wearing a black and white summer dress and her teeth were chattering. "Look at me," she said as she tried to talk, her mouth barely able to form the words, her lower jaw shaking. "It's not that cold."

We were in the old neighbourhood. The street was dark and narrow with shops on either side, and many people. I was asking my usual questions and she was doing her best to answer them.

"Look," she said again, and pointed to her lips which were shaking uncontrollably.

I nodded, drew my jacket tight, mentioned how much warmer it had been on the way to the cafe, my voice friendly enough but without the intonations of affection and interest, the rhythms of sympathy, the animation of friendship.

We entered the subway and felt warm again. She waited for my train to come, and tried to redeem herself and distance herself simultaneously. I asked about Danny and she answered. She went on and on. She talked about his job, her job, how little time each of them had for themselves. Almost before she finished, I asked about her children. Again she talked.

"I don't mean to brag," she said, helpless against the desire to brag, "but Victoria is so verbal."

Doing to her children and for herself what her mother had done to her and for herself.

"So verbal, so precocious. I don't say this to everyone." And she listed the words that Victoria already knew.

She still shivered occasionally. She must have known why I didn't call any more, aware of the reasons while inventing others in a self-defence that was both pathetic and dignified. She never asked what went wrong. Never begged for explanations (dignified even in her begging: her persistence as she continued to call and extend invitations).

We stood in the subway station – one in a black and white dress, the other in a warm jacket – one hurt and pale, the other triumphant in the indifference which had taken so long to acquire. We appeared to be friends. But a close observer would have seen how static we were, rooted in a determination not to have a scene, not to allow the other to cause hurt. Standing, waiting for my train to come in.

RICK MADDOCKS

Lessons from the Sputnik Diner

I learned about death in the kitchen. From the flies that kamikazed into the hot plate: *tsss!* From the cockroaches that scuttled under the sacks of rice when I opened the walk-in cupboard door. The rotten vegetables sitting out back in the dumpster, sucking in the flies. The shrimp curled up in the freezer like embryos. Most of all I learned about death from Marcel. One night, about closing time, a bat got in through the window and flapped about under the fluorescent lights. I hit the floor, wrapped my hair in a used napkin. I could hear Donna scream-laughing from the other side of the door. Then Marcel came running in with a baking sheet and spiked the bat into the deep fat fryer. Ethel Merman singing "Whole Lotta Love" in a vat of boiling oil. I remember Marcel smiling, like he'd won a prize.

Death: whenever I broke a dish or fucked up an order, Marcel would kick the swinging door open and scream, "Jack, I'm going to *keel* you!"

"My name's Rick."

"My name's Rick. What the fuck it matter to me. I still going to *keel* you, Jack!"

By now the spatula was shaking over his head and he was blistered in sweat. Red face. White hair shooting sparks out his hair net.

"Don't look him in the eye," Paul the Dishwasher said.

"Shut up that mouth, Jack." The spatula now pointed at Paul's back.

77

I snuck a look over at Paul. Pimply kid. Dungeons and Dragons type. He was leaning over the big stainless steel sink, facing the wall, and his shoulders were shaking. I bit my lip, started shredding the lettuce. But when I saw Marcel still glaring at us, chin up like Marlon Brando, I couldn't help snorting. Bad habit. Paul's shoulders were shaking lots now. He was laughing donkey-style.

Marcel jumped for him, snatched a dirty plate out of his hand, and smashed it against the floor: "Now you clean up *two* plates, dishpig! *You!*" He pointed at me. "Turn that radio down and why no hair net on that mess?"

I put the tape deck on pause, turning it down being sacrilege: "Funk #49" by the James Gang. Joe Walsh when he could still play guitar half-sober. Ugly southern distortion. I turned back and stared at the fishnet on Marcel's head. Him nodding slow, waiting for an answer.

"Hey, Marcel."

"What?"

"Two minutes for looking so good."

He ignored Paul donkey-laughing into the sink. Gave me a tap on the head with his spatula instead and then smiled mean: "You funny guy, eh? Yeah, pretty soon you be funny dead guy." He kicked the door open again, whispering through his teeth: "I *keel* you, Jack. Oh, yes . . ."

When the door swung back open, Donna walked in with a too-tight blouse and a half-eaten Reuben.

"You guys shouldn't talk to him like that. He's upset."

"No shit," I said.

"Vivien's threatening to chop off her ring finger. Says she's sick of waiting for Marcel to put something shiny round it."

"If she does," Paul said, "ask her if I can have it for science class."

Me and Donna raised our eyebrows at each other. Hers were thicker than mine. She shoved the plate of Reuben down on the counter and put her hands on her hips.

"Too much sauerkraut."

"It's a Reuben sandwich."

"The woman's a bitch. I'm not going to go back out there and tell her it's a Reuben sandwich."

"Tell her she's a bitch then."

Donna's eyebrows kinked up like black squirrels. Then her arms dropped and she laughed, kid-style, teeth biting her bottom lip while the rest of her face blushed over. I always felt embarrassed when she did this. It didn't go with her body, the short black hair curled tight around her head. She gave me a soft hip-check and said: "Ham and Eggs, a Western, and Marcel says if you don't wear a net at least put your hair in a ponytail."

"Yes'm."

She swept up a couple of new orders and waltzed out again. I watched the zipper on her hip jangle. And her legs: they were freshly shaven because each pore was a pin-prick of blood. When the door swung back and forth I could hear strains of "Blue Bayou" on the juke box, Marcel saying "Not bad for a blind guy," and someone laughing after it. My ass was still stinging from her pinch.

"I got one thing to say to you," Paul said.

"Huh?"

"Hospital."

Paul always said some pretty weird things. Half the time I'd just nod. This time I laughed dumb, tried to wipe the bacon grease from my hair. I felt something else, sticky, on my hand and forehead. When I looked down, the lettuce was soaked with red-black blood. There was the lettuce shredder still whirring round and here was my picking finger, hanging open by the tendons.

"Hospital," I said.

Marcel opened the Sputnik Diner during the Hagersville Tire Fire of 1989. Said it was an act of God started the restaurant and a bunch of *steenk*ing kids started the fire. His grand opening sign said: WHY GO TO A BUNCH OF BURNING TIRES IN HAGERS-VILLE WHEN YOU CAN GO TO THE MOON? EAT AT THE SPUT-NIK. It covered both windows and the door; people had to crawl under it to get inside. I think most people only read as far as MOON anyway, because the diner never was Grand Central

Station. When Marcel bought the place, a family was renting the upstairs apartment – a woman called Vivien, little boy and girl. Marcel didn't have the heart to kick them out, so for the first couple of weeks he slept on the black and white diamonds of the diner floor. Suitcase for a pillow, old menus for a blanket. One night Vivien felt so sorry for him she let him come up and share her fold-out couch. The next morning he woke up to a fingernail tracing the edges of his pubic hair. Four years later and he was still waking up with her beside him, though he'd bought a Craft-matic bed during the Gulf War.

Nowadays he only went upstairs if he was drunk. Most after-noons he hung the CLOSED sign up in the window, sat behind the counter with his gin and lemonade, and jawed with George and George, the couple of old pisspots grinning across from him. They laughed at everything he said as long as the booze kept coming, even if he told them he had prostate cancer. When Vivien came down, the laughing would stop: shaky hands run-ning through greasy hair, glasses of gin and lemonade getting shoved under the counter. She'd walk straight for the cutlery drawers, pull out a Ginsu knife and hold it at arm's length.

"Here."

"What?"

"Here. Why don't you get it over with?"

"Aw, Vivvy, not again . . ."

"Just drive it in right here." She pounded her chest. "Right through these tits you used to rub your fucking frog face in!"

"Vivvy, Vivvy, why you say these things? In front of my guests."

"Your guests, my ass! Look at them: they're starting to shake *now*. They've had to hide their drinks from me for thirty seconds."

"Aw, no, Vivvy. You're wrong."

"Fucking right, I'm wrong. Been wrong ever since you walked in with that suitcase and that stupid white hair on your head. Wrong waiting for four years – *four fucking years!* – for you to come around and at least call the kids by their real names. Sean was waiting for you to come up and play Super Mario with him ever since he got home from school. And here you are pissed with these losers and he's asleep on the floor with the joystick still in his hand."

"Good kid, that Sean."

"How would *you* know? You're too busy pissing money down the drain with one hand and hiring those curvy little slut waitresses with the other. And besides, his name is Lance."

"Ouch," said George.

Marcel sighed, turned an it's-the-gin-talking smile on Vivien. All he saw was the cash register and soft-drink fountain. He heard the thud of footsteps and then a door slamming upstairs.

"Marcel."

"Yes, George."

"That woman's got a mouth on her."

"You're right there."

"Yeah," said George. "And she's got a face for chopping wood on too."

"You say that again, my very best friend, and I will *keel* you."

That night Marcel clambered up the stairs, his hands fumbling for the walls in the darkness. The apartment door was locked. When his eyes adjusted, he saw the Ginsu knife stuck in the wood just above the peephole. He pressed his back against the door and slid down to his knees, tears lapping over his face.

"Fucking fingernail," he said.

Least that's what Donna told me.

"Marcel tells me everything," she said. "I mean *everything*."

On slow mornings in the Sputnik, we sat at a window booth, nursing coffees and praying no more customers came in. I usually listened as she filled me in, staring at the circuit between her neck and her face: happy and freckled. But her eyelashes were monsters. Small birds could use them as springboards, dive right in her coffee cup. Sometimes I got tangled up in them. Had to shake my head hard, tell her to start over again.

"I said Marcel came down here from Quebec."

"Surprise, surprise. Don't you hear him dinging the bell every four seconds so he can shout out he's the former Québécois Arm Wrestling Champion?"

"Smartass. Thing is, he's wanted." She was bent over the table now, whispering. When she blinked I felt the slightest draught, "His name isn't Marcel," she said, "it's something *La*-something."

"Guy Lafleur?"

She slapped my arm. Spilt coffee. "That's a baseball player or something, isn't it." Donna had those eyelashes and a white blouse that strained full when she bent over the tables, but she had an imagination on her. "Notice he doesn't have a driver's licence, how he always pays for stuff in cash? They say he's got a wife back there, too."

I shook my head and looked out the window. Her reflection was spread out against the parking meters, staring wide-eyed at me, nodding. We both looked over at the counter where Marcel was talking confidential over a cigarette with George and George, waving the smoke in their faces. Them laughing, hands fidgety.

"You think he *keeled* someone?" I said. She ignored that.

"This one time, before you started here," she whispered, "I saw him out back by the dumpster with these two guys in suits – never seen them before – and he opened up this briefcase. Full of money. When one of those guys zipped it up and shook his hand, Marcel saw me in a window, just for a second. I was shitting. He never said anything about it though."

Marcel had stopped jawing with George and George; he was giving us the evil eye now. I nodded at him, watched his face get a bit pink.

"Get your ass out of gears, Jack. I don't pay you for the chatting up of girls."

I learned about carrots by the juke box.

Except for the Georges and a big Dutchman called Noel, every guy who walked into the Sputnik had the same name.

Ninety-year-old Jack from the Greyhound station. Also known as *That Old Bastard*. Ordered the Lunch Special #1 every day of the week, never failing to bitch that his ice water was too cold. Walked with two canes. If you went to the bus station at noon, you'd have to spend a good two hours on the ripped red leather couch in the "lobby" before That Old Bastard walked the single block back from his Sputnik lunch.

Black Jack. Swaggered in the door every morning with blonde, dyed-black hair, a black fringe leather jacket, and snakeskin boots, black. Also two perfect blonde little boys holding tight to each hand. Only thing they said was daddy daddy daddy can we have juice. He'd poke a stub of white bread into a sunnyside up and read the *Toronto Sun* in silence. Export "A" cigarette always lit in the bread-mopping hand. "Crazy Little Thing Called Love" always on the juke box. Alias *Hard-to-Figure Jack*.

Call the Cops Jack. A middle-aged motorcycle guy with hair so thin and blonde he'd pass for the grandfather of Black Jack's kids. Taught his own son to box from an early age. Kept him locked in the garage for the whole of August '76, opening the door every four hours to "pound the living shit out of the boy." This story he told with his chin up and his paw curled round a black coffee: "Turned the little crud into a man." I think his son was serving a third term in Millhaven Penitentiary.

Heart Attack Jack. This name covered several regulars.

Whenever Marcel dinged the bell and called out "*Jack!* Continental breakfast!" ten or more men would rush to the counter with their receipt. Sometimes fights would break out, blood and HP sauce all over the floor's black and white diamonds. Big Noel would have to step in then, laughing and choking back coffee. Noel was kind of a freelance bouncer. An electrician by trade, he spent his nights at the Melbourne Hotel, mornings at the Sputnik, afternoons at the welfare office. He had the body of a bear, but was giddy as a cheerleader. If anybody made a wisecrack or even looked at him goofy, Noel started giggling. Only thing is, he always ate raw carrots alongside his bacon and eggs. At least once a week, someone would notice him get out of his chair quietly and walk to the washroom, his hand round his throat.

"S'matter Noel? You chokin'?"

Nod nod, yes yes.

"It's those carrots, Noel."

Nod nod.

Once I caught him all purple in the face, leaning on the juke box. I hurdled the counter and dove right into the Heimlich, but he was too huge: my hands couldn't reach round the other side. Two other men tried before the chunk of carrot shot out and splatted on the Wurlitzer logo. "You've Got a Friend" by James Taylor was playing. Noel started to giggle.

It got so whenever Noel sat down with his bacon and eggs and raw carrots, Marcel stood back and surveyed the room for the man with the longest arms: "Hey, *Jack!*"

I learned to play guitar in Donna's bedroom, between the butter-flies and ice.

One Sunday I got off early because Marcel was sick of seeing my *heepy* face. I hung around the place just to bug him, pouring quarters in the juke box, whipping my hair round to the Talking Heads, shouting along to the 365-degree part in "Burning Down the House." Finally he said: "Okay. I make you a deal, Jack: you play that song one more time, I get to punch you in the face."

I made like I didn't hear him, just watched Donna making con-versation with the customers: "I thought you had a heart attack last week, Charlie! . . . Is that right? . . . Well, no sex for you for a while, eh? . . ." Charlie must've been at least seventy-five.

I watched her lean over the empty table, her tongue sticking out the side of her mouth as she wiped. Half an hour later my tongue was doing the same: me tugging at the zipper on her skirt, she breathing into my mouth, her hand a spider inside my jeans. When she saw my plaid boxers she laughed kid-style. Shut up shut up. Thick black hairs jabbed out from her panties like calligraphy. For a second I had this image of Marcel naked on his Craftmatic. It went away when I fell on top of her and the bed, our ankles tangled up in denim and black cotton.

She was sighing somebody else's name when I heard the noise under the bed. Hollow, like a boat. Then a spring popped out of the mattress, dragged across strings. An open chord. I slipped out of her and leaned over the side, dragged out the hunk of wood and metal.

"It was my father's," she said, and rolled over, scooping an ice cube from the glass on the floor. She placed the ice in between her legs and closed her eyes. Her breasts, in the light, looked pock-marked, like fallen dough. On the wall behind them, there was a glass case: butterflies pinned to a white background. One had fallen and lay crumpled on the bottom, the pin still sticking through its dry black shell. I kneeled down on the carpet, strummed the open strings until my penis was caked dry and only a few beads of water glistened on her wiry hair.

"It was your father's."

"Hmmm?" she said, opening her eyes.

"I said it *was* your father's."

"Yes."

In two weeks I'd learned the chords G, D, C, and A major and minor. I played "Tequila Sunrise" till my fingertips turned green from the rusted copper-bound strings. I was halfway through the second verse one night, getting to the "hollow feeling" line, when Donna jumped off the bed, saying she hated the Eagles and was going out for ice.

I learned about *Ben Hur* by the window. Donna's white blouse was in my face, she was filling up my coffee. "Marcel and me would be lovers if he wasn't so old." I told her not to say stuff like that while I was eating. When she was done with another order, she slid into the booth and smiled across from me. "I got him into bed once."

"*What?*"

Vivien and the kids were away one weekend. Marcel was giddy as Noel the Dutchman, shuffling along to "Blue Bayou," twirling Donna around whenever she came by with a menu or a plate of steaming stuff. Him singing along with the Wurlitzer in a French-Canadian accent. After the last chorus he'd turn to a George, smoke dangling. "Not bad for a blind guy, that Roy Orbeeson."

Marcel closed the place at ten o'clock that morning, broke out the gin and lemonade, and let the juke box play till nobody wanted to go back to Blue Bayou ever. Around midnight, Donna came back to the Sputnik to check up on him. He was blinking

slow at the TV, George and George slumped unconscious over
the counter across from him. His face looked thin, naked. "They
got this machine," he said, never taking his eyes off the screen.
"It's a vacuum *clee*ner and it cuts your hair."

Donna helped him up the stairs, his body surprisingly light.
At the door Marcel checked for the Ginsu knife, and then nodded, frowning: "It's okay, we go in." Donna laughed too loud and
stood in the doorway, watching him trying to take his shoes off.
When he started using his teeth, she got down on her knees and
pushed his face out of the way.

"Donna, my waitress."

"Hmmm?"

"*Ben Hur.*"

"Ben who?"

"No no no no no. *Ben Hur:* greatest movie of all times.
Romans and horses and Jesus and that guy who was Moses. Carl-
ton Weston. You got to watch this man, people of your gen'ration.
If I was a woman . . ."

"Gross," Donna said. "Now let's getcha to bed."

"Nope. You watch it with me tonight. On VHS."

She looked around, sighed okay: "Where's the machine?"

"Bedroom." He shrugged and closed his eyes, smiling.

Donna slid the tape in, waited for it to rewind. "Marcel," she
said, gazing at the static screen. "Why'd you call it the Sputnik
Diner?"

"Because this country. I am proud for being Canadian."

"But Sputnik was a Russian spaceship or something."

"Tell me lies. It's the proper name for that arm in space with
CANADA on it. I'm from east of Gatineau. Proud for this country. I know . . . about the science."

Donna fixed her eyes on the TV till the letter-box screen flickered up and then the credits started to roll in yellow and red
Technicolor: "Okay, you happy now, spaceman?"

When she turned around, Marcel was sprawled out on the
Craftmatic, completely naked. Little white sparks of hair shot
out from between his thighs. His cock looked malnourished. He
was rocking side to side, and he was crying.

"The woman I live with, I don't love her."

"I know, Marcel."

"I pack my suitcase twelve times. Had it waiting under the counter, ready for going. But when I go to pick it up, my hand it reaches for the gin instead."

Donna put her hand on his knee; he took it and held it like money.

"Her face," he said, opening wet, serious eyes: "You can chop wood on it."

He fell asleep mumbling the number thirteen and something about hamburgers. Donna spread a blanket over him, tucked it under his feet, and turned the volume way up on the TV.

"Maybe he dreamt about Romans that night," she said.

"Marcel. Hire a new waitress. A skinny one."

Vivien's first words after she dumped her kids and weekend baggage onto the floor. Marcel obliged, no questions asked. He took on the first girl who walked in the Sputnik's door. You could hear Cheryl before you saw her. Bracelets jangled from her wrists and ankles, long dangly earrings made from metal and bone whistled by her shoulders when she moved. She was a porch full of wind chimes. But the rest of her was quiet. If Donna's voice didn't know what to do with itself, Cheryl's face was fenced in with barbed wire, her laugh a squeak with a hand in front of it. Donna's body an extrovert; Cheryl's thin-wristed and brown, attracted to the outskirts of rooms. And the new girl's hair was long, brown and dangerous. On a hot day, there was always the chance it would get tangled up in one of the metal fans dotted round the diner.

Donna and Cheryl–Cheryl and Donna. Too opposite for real life. From my window booth, I watched the differences happen as Cheryl moved over the black and white diamonds, her hips jack-knifing past chairs and elbows. Me making a list of these things.

"Watcha writing?"

"Nothing."

Tsss! Marcel was watching the differences too, flipping bacon behind the counter. Peameal. I could smell it clear across the room. I could see his teeth, yellow from cigarettes, smiling at his girls through the grease and smoke. *Done good*, he was thinking: *Hired a new waitress, just like Vivvy said*. Problem was he kept Donna on the payroll, slating her on the same shift as Cheryl most days. Now Vivien stood in the kitchen door with an electrical storm crackling over her head and stared through Marcel's back, past the two Georges, to the Jekyll and Hyde waitresses pirouetting on the diner floor.

I learned about strawberries from Amburger. I was left in charge on Sunday morning, frying up paprika hash browns and sausage on Marcel's personalized flat-top behind the counter. The Stones pouting out "Emotional Rescue" from the Wurlitzer, me doing my best Mick Jagger impression. No Georges around to make fun of me. Vivien sleeping upstairs. Donna wiping tables in the corner. I'd just twirled around to slap the bell when in walks six feet of fake fur, shocking pink and hips.

Ding! She had black leather boots that funnelled up her thighs. After that it was pink spandex clammed tight round her pelvis, gold ring in her navel, and a furry vest sort of thing that left the sides of her breasts bare. Her hair was dying to stay blonde. And she was carrying a green box full of strawberries.

"Hi, honey. Marcel around?"

"Hi."

"Hi. Is Marcel around?"

"No."

She laughed low and I was ten years old again.

"He still living with Mother Teresa?" she said, pointing at the ceiling.

I pictured a Ginsu knife in Marcel's chest. "Yes."

She laughed again. Tongue against teeth. Behind her, Donna was wiping the same table she'd been doing five minutes ago. Eyebrows on fire, scowling at me. I made a move to push my hair out of my face, forgot it was in a hair net.

The woman set the strawberries down and leaned over the counter. She smelled of menthol cigarettes, Grand Marnier.

"Tell him Amber's at the Pump tonight." She plucked a strawberry from the pile, worked it between her lips, then punished it

between her teeth. I nodded stupid in my hair net: *Okay*. I
smelled burning. When she walked out the door, I could see day-
light through the gap at the top of her thighs.

Not ten minutes later, Marcel floated in with his arm draped
round Noel the Dutchman's shoulder. I was still Brillo-padding
the black chunks of hash brown from the flat-top, erection fad-
ing. All Noel said was: "Three whisky doubles on the rocks . . .
he fall down . . . three whisky doubles on the rocks . . . he fall
down again." He eased Marcel into a window booth while
Donna got coffee. Marcel slumped over, arm wrestling the air.

"Hey Marce," I said, carrying the strawberries waiter-style to
the table: "Some chick called Amber came by and brought you
these."

I felt a sharp stab in my ribs. Donna's elbow. Marcel slapped
his arm down on the table and sat up straight. He ignored the
coffee Donna shoved in front of him, grabbed the box of strawberries in his massive hands, and stared milky at me:
"Amburger?"

I nodded. Close enough.

A smile spread across his face like jam: "*Am*burger."

"You shouldn't have told him," Donna said, scooping another
ice cube out of her glass and running it up the inside of her
thigh. I watched a silver trail trickle down around the back of her
leg. I leaned over the bed, my knees sore on the carpet, and
lapped it up slow with the tip of my tongue. Liquid. She started
wrapping my hair around her fist, her own hair black and rough
against my cheek.

"Why, what's the deal with *Am*burger?"

"Don't know what you're saying."

"Okay," I said. "I'll rephrase: what did Marcel tell you about
this stripper called Amber?"

"Your mouth's too full. Ask me later."

Later her fingertips were drumming her pillow absently;
mine were green and busy with the guitar. I had a few more
chords under my belt now: E major and minor, F, B minor. Problem was I'd lost all feeling in my picking finger. The stitches
from the lettuce shredder were still buried in there. My skin had

grown thick over the nylon thread. Now I had to watch my strumming hand the whole time I played, otherwise I'd be fumbling at air. (Donna noticed this in bed too.) I still managed "Play with Fire" though, and would've finished "Strawberry Fields Forever" if she hadn't thrown the ice water in my face while I was doing an extra-nasal John Lennon: *No one, I think, is in my tree . . .*

She sat up, her breasts slouching over her belly. "Ever since you picked up that thing our fucking's gotten, I don't know, *efficient*."

I stood up, shook the ice out the guitar, then laid it careful across the foot of the bed and walked to the door. "Look."

"Hmmm?" She stared expressionless at me, wet and hairy by the light switch.

"Bet you five bucks my fingertips glow in the dark."

By the time I flicked the switch back on, the guitar had gone *brummm!* against the floor. Donna was bundled under the covers, facing the wall. I looked in the butterfly case for her reflection, but all I could see was the dead insects.

I learned about flukes from Cheryl. My hands were rich with liver and onions and she was dusting another broken plate into the garbage. Her body sighed. Out of the corner of my eye I saw a long, dark leg slip out her skirt, a scar visible on the knee. I waited for her jewellery to stop singing, then nodded towards the garbage can.

"Which order was that? The Reuben?"

"Not Reuben," she said, "reuben. It's a small 'r'."

Her face was serious.

At lunchtime, after she polished off a bowl of minestrone soup, I gave her the Sputnik questionnaire: (a) so where you from and (b) what the hell are you doing *here*?

a) *Newfoundland.*

b) *My grandmother. She's dying.*

She stirred her coffee counterclockwise and stared out the window. Eyes like blue granite. A car floated by in her pupils. I felt my hand, damp, tighten around my cup. Wanted to say something like *my coffee's cold*, but my eyes got caught up in a chain dangling shiny in the V of her blouse, a silver whale's tail threaded onto it.

"It's my fluke," she said, pulling it away from her skin. I nodded, cleared my throat a bit loud. Her watching me watching her. She plucked a strand of hair from her tongue, let it fall slow-motion into the tin ashtray, then stared down at her coffee. Me surprised when she kept talking, twirling the fluke between her long, shellacked fingernails.

"I used to go to this little fishing village about a half hour south of St. John's. Ferryland. Ever heard of it? *Any*way, the wind off the coast there always smelled of pine trees. Always. And there was this cove where maybe twenty humpbacks used to come and . . . umm . . . play. We'd sit at the front of the boat and dangle our feet over the edge. You could see them swim under the boat and then surface right beside you. Perfect. Then. *psssh!* They'd bring their flukes up out the water and it was like they were waving at you. Showoffs, I thought. Then I read in *National Geographic* or something that that's how they tell each other apart. Individuals. No two flukes are the same. Sort of a whale fingerprint."

She looked back out the window and, nodding quiet to herself, placed the fluke flat on her chest. I swallowed a mouthful of cold coffee.

"A Chevy Impala just cruised straight through your left eye," I said.

I learned about rodents in Marcel's apartment. Marcel was taking Vivien and the kids to a trailer park north of Toronto; he asked Donna to mind the place for the weekend. Vivien wasn't too comfortable with the idea. Her exact words: "I'd rather drink Tabasco in hell than have that slut sleeping in my bed." Marcel, making sure he stood between her and the cutlery drawers, said: "It's okay, Vivvy. We'll drop you off at the CN Tower with some buynoculars so you can stand up there and watch all the goings-on down here."

On Saturday night, I closed the Sputnik early and went upstairs, guitar slung over my shoulder. (Almost had the 6/4 timing to "Sweet Thing" figured out, dead finger and all.) When I opened the door, Donna and Cheryl were running round the apartment, screaming. I thought they were pissed until a bat swooped down, ears and teeth an inch from my face. I swung the guitar round, missed, then dropped to the floor. "Wimp," Cheryl said. While Donna was busy jumping on and off the bed, Cheryl caught the bat in a patchwork quilt and swung the bundle into the corner. Then our breathing died down and we could hear this noise, *crick-crick-crick* like a geiger counter, moving along the baseboards. I said "Shit." Donna laughed kid-style. Cheryl kicked a chair out of the way and came out of the corner a minute later with the bat in her hands: "Open the window."

I was still flat on the carpet, too impressed to move. She nudged the window open herself, but when she threw the thing out over Robinson Street, she knocked a plant from the sill. A second later we heard it crash against the sidewalk. Cheryl shrugged, closed the window, and dusted off her hands: "No casualties." I pictured a Ginsu knife in her chest.

Three more bats flew into Marcel's apartment that night. After the second one we just left the windows open, hoping they could find their own way out. Later we rummaged through Marcel's movie collection, bypassing *Ben Hur* and settling on *The Good, the Bad, and the Ugly*. Even before the *Good* saved the *Ugly* from his first hanging, Cheryl fell asleep on the floor in front of me. Her hair spilled across the rug like soft coral. In the darkness I worked it, silky, between my bare toes. Donna, bored with the movie, went to the freezer for a glass of ice. She came back from the kitchen with her T-shirt off, balled up in her hand. Curly hairs were visible outside the V of her panties. Her tits looked disappointed. She said: "I think I'd like to go to Mexico."

"Actually," I said, "they made these films in Italy. Hence the term Spaghetti Western."

"I don't give a shit where they were made."

We spent the rest of the night on the Craftmatic: Clint Eastwood squinting on the TV, bats making casual flights around the apartment, my cock dreaming in Donna's cold mouth and my feet in Cheryl's hair.

Home from the trailer park the next morning, Vivien could

only find two faults with the place: (1) The missing African violet and (2) The stale glass of water beside the bed.

I learned about chemical reactions from Paul the Dishwasher. One morning Marcel came in the kitchen nursing a hangover. Wasn't in there two seconds before he snapped at Paul: "Turn down that racket, and after you done them plates, *cleen* out the sink, and *good!*" The big steel basin was corroded, a ring of brown rust sleeping there for years now. Paul plugged it up and dumped in a whole bottle of Windex. I was fixing up a Sputnik Omelette, sprinkling cheese, onions, and green peppers into the pan. Humming along to "Chuck E.'s in Love" on the Classic Hits station. Before the first chorus hit, Paul poured something else into the sink, and then donkey-laughed.

"S'up, Paul?"

"Check this out," he said, waving me over. I was halfway across the kitchen floor when a blue mushroom cloud plumed out the sink. Went up my nostrils like razor blades. I saw Paul's legs buckle, then the back of his skull go smack against the tiles. Next thing I knew, I was dragging him from the basin, trying to slap him back to life, and Marcel was already peeling me away from the kid like I was papier-mâché.

"Don't hit him when he is out like that, Jack."

I nodded. Okay.

"Let the little guy's body handle it. It'll know when to wake up."

I looked at Marcel dumb. Never heard him talk so quiet and sensical.

"It'll know," he said, tapping me soft on the shoulder, nodding.

For the next few minutes we said nothing, just stared down at the zonked-out teenager. Me kneeling on the tiles, Marcel standing behind me, spatula folded in his arms. Under the fluorescent lights, the walls began to hum lime green. Objects in the room started losing their names, got naked. Pretty soon I was wiping my hands on my jeans. Behind me the former arm wrestling champion of Quebec was slapping a cooking utensil against his chest in hypnotic rhythm. The Sputnik Omelette was burnt black as cancer. Rickie Lee Jones was whining *Cos* . . . *Chuck E.'s-inlovewiththelittlegi-irrlll* . . . *who's singing this song*. And there was something about Paul's face under the lights, too. Flaky, almost green. I half expected his pimples to start sprouting flowers.

Then his eyelids flickered. Marcel dropped the spatula and knelt down beside me, propping up Paul's head, his big red fingers in the boy's greasy hair. Me guilty from seeing this intimate gesture. He tapped Paul lightly on the cheek. When Paul's eyes rolled open, squinting against the lights, Marcel slapped him a couple more times, then punched him square on the nose: "You *lee*ttel *ee*diot! What the fuck you think you doing?!"

Before he could throw another punch I got him in a headlock, connected with a right and then – *kungg!!!* – an accidental knee to the balls. Marcel's face blanched. He squirmed loose, grabbed a fistful of my hair, then went for the throat, shaking me like a bottle of World Series champagne. I snapped up the spatula, held it over my head guillotine-style. By now sinews were electrical cables popping out of Marcel's arms. His hair net had slipped sideways off his head and his face was glaring red back at me: "I will *keel* you, Jack . . . this time . . . *Keeel* you!"

Then, for a moment, I heard wind chimes. They danced in and out of the room, just above our breathing and swearing. Froze me long enough for the door to swing open and something cold to touch my neck. Vivien: Ginsu pressed flat against my skin. Out the corner of my eye, I saw Donna and Cheryl over by the steam table, trying not to look. Then I heard giggling; the next thing Big Noel grabbed me under the arms, plucked me off Marcel, and sat me up on the counter like I was a three-year-old. I looked around the room and everyone else was crying. (Except for Paul: he was pinned under Marcel, out cold again. When he came to, he only had one thing to say and I've never seen him since.) Before I knew it I was spilling tears, too, saying "I'm sorry, I'm *sorry*." Then I realized our eyes were watering from Paul's sink cocktail.

I learned about inefficient sex on the stairs. On a Tuesday afternoon I went to the Sputnik to pick up my last cheque. Marcel wasn't around. Vivien, hot and flustered behind the counter, threw me an envelope and said: "Hang on, you. Got something else upstairs."

I waited at the counter, the Georges sitting a few stools down from me. They both grinned, eyes bloodshot over their morning bottles of Budweiser: "Ya leaving us, young guy?" George asked.

"Yes, George."

"He's going to be a rock 'n' roller," George said. "Be the next Paul Anka."

"That right?" George laughed, his head bobbing between his shoulders.

"Fuck off, George," I said, but I was laughing too.

Then Vivien came back out the swinging door with a T-shirt scrunched up in her hand: "Found it under the couch cushions. Yours, I expect."

I smiled: "Thanks, Vivvy." As I walked out across the black and white tiles, "Sea of Love" wobbled from the Wurlitzer. I could feel Vivien's eyes dissecting my back. I stopped outside the window and, cranking up a fake smile, waved through the sign. But she was looking away, talking snarky to one of the Georges. Her greying hair was stuck flat to her forehead, almost black with sweat.

Click. The light was blown out in the entrance to Donna's apartment. This meant blackness, even in the daytime. At the foot of the stairs, I heard Donna sighing out my name. I ran up a couple of steps, stumbling over a bundle of newspapers, then heard her voice again. I stood outside the door, listening: knock. Knock. Squeak. Knock. Squeak. My name being called again. Knock. Quiet tinkle of glass. After that, all I heard was a fan whirring in the darkness above me, a car horn outside. I draped the T-shirt neatly over the doorknob and walked slow down the blackened stairs.

I learned about death on a cordless phone. *The Ten Commandments* was the CBC Late Movie and I was splayed out on the couch, Donna's voice crackling in my ear. She was in Albuquerque, New Mexico. Said she'd found this AT&T calling card on the bus station floor: "So here I am calling *you!*" She asked me if I'd gotten any of the postcards she sent. I said no. Then she told me about Marcel.

"It was awful, Rick. The last time I saw him, he was sprawled out in the back seat of a cab outside the Sputnik. He had his suitcase with him and a bottle of gin and he was spilling it all over the place. Crying. And he kept saying how he didn't want to be hurting anyone, but Amburger was waiting for him at the Zanzibar in Toronto. I couldn't stop from crying. I don't know, his hair was so white. I could see clear through it, see his scalp. You know the last thing he said?" A shaky laugh. "Drive, Jack."

I heard her voice catching over the fibre optic fine, then she said: "I went back the next day and there was this guy in a three-piece suit asking where Marcel was. He told me how much money Marce owed some people. *Some people*, what the fuck does that mean? I said I didn't know anything about it. Then first thing Vivien does when I walk in the door is fire me. Canned Cheryl, too. Bitch. Did you ever see her after you quit?"

"Who?"

"Vivien."

"No."

"Well, she took off too, after nobody but the Georges kept coming to the place. Just packed up the kids and left. God knows where. Gave all Marcel's movies and shit to the Salvation Army."

She gave me time to say something. In the silence I could hear the ghost of another conversation, a pair of southern voices. Something about a fire.

"Oh, and Noel the Dutchman died."

"What?"

"Yeah. Few days after Marcel skipped town. Choked to death halfway to the bathroom."

"The carrots."

"No," she said. "Diamond ring. It must've fallen into the scrambled eggs or something. When the coroner brought it back the next day, no one claimed it. Then, get this, Vivien tried it on and it was a perfect fit."

"No."

"Uh-huh."

Awkward silence. She told me about the food in the Youth
Hostel, some ("get this") Russian guy she'd met, and a fat lady
who kept picking her up and dancing with her "like I was a frig-
ging rag doll!"

After that, her voice was far away and I started saying "yeah"
in all the wrong places. Switching the phone to the other ear, I
said: "Look, I'd better go. This thing must be costing you a
mint."

"No, it's all right. It's on the calling card, remember?"

"Yeah, but I really should go. Kinda busy."

"Guitar, right?"

"Huh?"

"Still playing that damn guitar?"

"Oh, yeah."

When I hung up she was still saying goodbye. I clicked the
telephone off and set it down on the coffee table. A pile of postcards smattered to the floor. Charlton Heston was standing in
front of me, six inches tall and gawking at a Technicolor burning bush. I stretched back out on the couch. In the darkness I pictured Marcel, white hair luminous as lightning, standing alone
at his personalized flat-top on the moon, still waiting for the
bacon to come down. A box of strawberries levitating half-
empty over the counter. *Ding!* I closed my eyes and rolled over.

"Don't put my fluke in your mouth," Cheryl said. "It'll rust."

ELYSE GASCO

Can You Wave Bye Bye, Baby?

It is surprisingly easy to run out of love. You do not chug or lurch suddenly like a car, coughing every few steps. You don't scream or bellow like the heaving hot water taps. If someone shook you side to side like a milk carton, they wouldn't know that you were almost out, down to the last drop. There is no warning. It is so sudden, you cannot imagine that it was ever there to begin with. Hardly anything else in the whole world disappears quite that easily, without a shudder. For the first two weeks when you held the baby in your arms you thought you felt something, something fishy maybe, the sensation you get when you hold a small guppy in your cupped hands and you can feel it twitching against the side of your palms, quick little flutters, desperate. Now, when you look at her face, her eyelids raw from crying, her fists curled under her chin as though in prayer, it is as though you swallowed a cold, round river stone. When you move, it rolls through your empty body, making you shiver. She is not feeding well. Your breasts are rocky and engorged. The best thing to do is to express yourself. You look down at her soft, unfinished head, and say: I don't think I will ever really love you.

The first time you do it, you are shivering so hard, tingling in all the creases of your skin, that after so long you can almost mistake it for a kind of hominess. The word *erotic* is in your head. Your heart is a heavy African drum, calling . . . calling . . . The humid night air settles like pollen on your bare arms, empty now, light, dusted with powder like moth wings. Walking away from your house, you are surprised at how far you get, that there is nothing physically holding you back, no elastic band, or choke chain and leash. You look like anyone, walking. What did you imagine? Your dress lifts a little in the breeze. Everything conspires to tease you. At the corner store you think the word *cigarette*. It comes so quickly after the word *erotic* that you think that maybe you are becoming yourself again. The moon is a full, pink flush. Outside the store with the red awning, teenagers balance on their bicycles, one hand leaning against the brick wall. The girls break their popsicles in half against the sharp corner of the wall and demonstrate a blow job, their lips and tongues staining dark purple. The group rides away laughing. A man stands with his dog. He is trying to light a match. The dog jumps up and the man curls his fingers into a neat fist and sends the dog hurling to the ground. Hey, you say, before you even realize that you are talking. The man turns to face you and his face seems damaged. His beard is uneven, his nose is flattened almost to his lip. Later, you will think that it is exactly how you imagined the face of an angel, challenging, ugly, filled with all the world's venomous wishes. Then take him, bitch, he says, throwing the leash at your feet. He turns away, running down the street, his long, thin black coat flapping like a crow. The dog doesn't move. He looks dazed and there is a bit of drool hanging from his black lips. You stand squinting after the shape of the man as though trying to read something on his back, trying to be a good witness, and think that really, people should be made to wear licence plates. No matter what, you ought to be able to track them down. You thought you had dried up. But as you are walking home, the dog walking slowly behind you, you feel pooling against the inside of your dress, trickling down between your ribs like sweat.

Newborns cry without tears. It is the only thing about them that is not liquid, and it surprises you. The point is that some things are just not yet fully formed and in a way you imagine that this is buying you some time. You lean over her crib and your face hovers just above hers like a horrible moon. Her arms flail and her legs kick in short jerky movements. You cannot figure out if she is simply panicking or if she is trying to throw herself right at you, propel herself with such force out of her crib that you are forced to catch her. You have seen many diaper commercials. Women with neat hair pulled back in headbands, their hands pink and clean, their rooms flooded with sunshine. You imagine yourself saying: Who's wet? Who needs a changing? Are you mommy's best girl? Are you? But you do not like the sound of your voice, high and sexless, like a cartoon character or someone going crazy, and all these one-sided conversations couldn't possibly prepare you for the arguments to come. You can tell already. She is willful. She will fight you tooth and bone. Already your nipples are cracked and bruised and she is only using her gums.

It gets easier. At first you muffle her cries by hiding in the bathroom, the shower running hot. You sit fully dressed on the edge of the tub and let the steam smother you. When your skin is damp and your cheeks are flushed, you open the door and the air makes you shiver. You make yourself cold and ready for her. You put her down on her stomach, her forehead pressed sadly into the mattress. Sometimes her head moves from side to side, denying everything. You do not like the way she looks up at you. Her eyes are abnormally huge and she hardly seems to blink. It is the only way she has to take you in. She has not heard the sound of your voice very often. She must think she is deaf. Maybe she cries for conversation. Soon, it seems she does not cry as often. She is trying to frighten you with her silence. Her hands will reach out and grab hold of your finger if you tease her with it. But this is an uncontrolled movement, involuntary. Her eyes are still adjusting. She cannot make out friend or foe. She reaches for the nearest thing at hand, but it has nothing to do with closeness.

The dog is taking the house apart. Each day you come home to find that something else has been eaten. A wicker basket, something you once made out of papier-mâché, an African mask, one high-heeled shoe. You know you should be angry, these are your things after all, but you find yourself humming as you pick up the scraps and threads of knickknacks, and strangely excited for the next casualty. You understand this anxiety, this need to strip everything bare, to rip through the sturdy right down to the essentials. Lately, your dreams are cloudy and white, and it seems that they are of nothing, a pale milky blankness where nothing exists. If you live without mirrors, all you might see of yourself all day are your hands, busy, using things, shaking, or just folded, quiet for a moment. In your dreams, when you look down, you do not even see your hands. You sweep away threads of a carpet you bought at a craft show, a charcoal drawing of your first well-proportioned nude, and a picture of your mother swimming, the only evidence of such a time. Your house seems to be expelling itself. Each time you look around it seems a great contraction, some kind of quake, has shaken loose your things, leaving them scattered and half torn all around. The dog drags a sweater across the floor. The empty arms dragging along the wood look like the legs of some strange, flappy deer and make the dog seem more savage than he really is. You ask yourself: What do I need? What do I need? But it seems that there is nothing that you miss. You love your dreams where nothing ever happens and pieces of you disappear, so that it seems that you might be becoming something close to breath.

It gets easier. When you leave her now, your heart slows right down by the end of your walkway and returns to its even tapping, or something more like a drip, a kind of Chinese water torture. Inside the house, the dog rages for you. Your house frays. Seams expose themselves. Fragments of materials – bedding, covers, diapers, and all types of everyday items, pieces of plastic Tupperware, spatulas, bathtub plugs and toilet plungers – everything scattered in colourful chunks and pieces like confetti or rice showered at some strange ceremony.

You drink at a neighbourhood bar. Silent television screens play European soccer games and the place is filled with reggae music. On Caribbean night, a man without a shirt offers to buy you a piña colada but it reminds you too much of milk spittle. Everyone looks so helpless to you, and every man calls you baby. Anyone waiting at home for you, baby? Can I get you anything, baby? It seems that no matter what you do you cannot get the smell of diapers or corn starch or that powdery infant scent from your hands. When you sweat it smells to you like sour milk. Some nights you dance by yourself on a small crowded dance floor, swaying back and forth, your body finally feeling lighter. You can feel your hip bones again as they bump accidentally against another dancer. You think that there is something right and fitting, worthy even, in taking up less and less space. One night, after you have had too much of something water-clear but potent, a man shares with you the size of his great heart. While he twirls a little mauve umbrella stuck inside his drink, he tells you long stories of all the women he has loved, and all the women he has yet to share his enormous passion with. He cannot help himself. He is filled to the brim. He orders himself another exotic drink. It is a strange bar, you think, where all the women like their shots straight up, and all the men are stirring cocktails. He seems lucky to you, this man, with his huge and generous heart. When he finally reaches out his clumsy hand and strokes your thigh, you tell this man: Sorry, I am fresh out of love, and your voice sounds almost innocent, like a dairy maid's, someone peach-faced, pert and healthy. A farmer's daughter who has just run out of eggs. A farmer's daughter glowing on her first trip to the city. The man says something about fresh . . . but you are already near the door. The bartender wipes your place clean and says: Goodbye, baby.

When you turn your corner you expect to see the red lights of fire engines, or waiting police cars, parked in front of your door, their mute lights spinning noiselessly, evil mimes, making the emergency seem too late. Each time, you are surprised by the stillness of your house, the ordinary way it sits beside the others on the block, the outside light on, making the bright blue of the door seem rich and inviting. It is always at this point that for one brief moment you think you feel something, a stirring, that makes you run the last half-block and fumble a little with the keys. But by the time you reach her, whatever it was is gone, and your heart has contracted back down into that knotty pit at the centre of some soft fruit. She lies in her crib with her eyes shut tight against you. She makes hardly any noises in her sleep. Each time you are stunned at her determination to stay alive. It seems impossible that she willed herself here, right into this world without any encouragement at all. Sometimes, you just want to shake her out of her dumb sleep, shake her and crush her tiny chest against yours until she cries in a terrible hopeless fear. But you grip the bars of the crib hard and hold your breath. It passes. It is better to feel this dark pitted nothingness than the other, the urge to damage and betray.

Your house is going through a kind of fall, an early autumn where everything is changing shape and colour, letting go, and piling up like leaves on the ground. Suddenly it is important to understand how everything works, the actual mechanics of everything you touch with your hands and pretend to know and understand, everything you take for granted in its everyday use, because lately you get the feeling that you have been fooling yourself, faking a sort of blasé familiarity with things, everyday objects that if your life depended on it you could probably never make for yourself. There must be one thing here that you could understand fully, then maybe others would follow in a natural logarithm. It just seems so wrong to make anything a part of your life, to make anything essential, if you cannot understand it, if you do not know how it works. Life is suddenly mathematics. First you multiply. Then you simplify, reduce. You ask yourself tough questions. What is my foundation? What have I built this self up from? What is this round wire thing hanging on my kitchen rack?

And so it begins. The toaster-oven. You don't know and so you unplug it. The glass you hold in your hand, supposedly recycled from old cola bottles, how is it made? could you do it yourself? And the answer is no, so you leave it on the counter top, beside the wilting plant you cannot name, that grows by sunlight and water but how exactly? Hand-painted plates, coffee mugs, aluminum foil, stuff in your fridge wrapped in plastic, made with real cheese products, everything, garlic, flour, teflon-coated pans . . . You make a great pile. Everything must go. You pass the dog on the way to your bedroom, chewing on the sleeve of a good silk blouse. You pause to consider. Well, there is a worm somewhere that spins out of its mouth? This thread called silk? And then the thread . . . But when you find that you can't go on, you bend to pat the animal's thick oily fur and say: Good dog.

At the health clinic, you sit in the waiting room and try to think up a name to call the baby in case someone asks. You listen to other women coo to their children. They stare down at their sleeping infants in portable car seats, baby slings, and wicker baskets, with full attention. They call out names. Henry. Lisa. Yasmine. Zach. But they seem so strange to you, these names, big labels that cannot fit, like a shirt too big, a bed sheet instead of a dress. How can something so small be a Hank? It is a joke to you, this naming, a game really, like throwing balled-up toilet paper against the wall, over and over again until finally it sticks. You become this name by habit, by the sheer force and will of those around you who insist on calling you something. When you call her, sometimes you call her Baby – Please Baby, please – but mostly she is just You: Hey, you with the dirty diaper. Just who do you think you are? Who do you think I am? And for a kind of comic relief, so that she might know that you do know how to smile: just wait till your father gets home. She can break your heart. All the power she hands you in one small fist. Animals are born almost ready to leave. They stand and drink and wobble and soon their mother disappears into a pack of identical looking gazelles, let's say, camouflaged by all the other perky white tails, who have turned their backs on their offspring. The shape of you, your cramped body, your tiny holes and escape hatches, your fragile bony home, everything you are, makes her frail and helpless. Doomed from the start.

She refuses your milk. The doctor tells you that she is underweight. It is not your imagination that he eyes you suspiciously and expresses concern about a nasty diaper rash, sticky in the folds of her raw skin, spreading. He wonders about allergies and asks you if you have a pet at home, and maybe because you do not think of the dog that way, as some kind of companion, something propels you to lie and you say no. He does not seem concerned that she is unnamed. He calls her little one. You do not watch as he measures her, or administers her vaccines, and she does not cry. Already she is trying to blend, to shade herself into the cool metal of the scale, or the long delicate fingers of the doctor, or the crisp white paper of the examining table. You do not notice when the doctor tries to hand her back to you. You are staring at the large tiles on the floor, counting the squares from your feet to the door, from your sandals to the doctor's leather loafers, from one end of the room to the other. He asks you if everything is all right. Do you have any questions? Is there anything you want to talk about? He must see the way you shrivel so obviously under his gaze, willing yourself to be trapped by this man, picking dog hairs from your black jeans and letting them fall onto the speckled linoleum floor. But for the first time in your life everyone wants to believe the best of you. He suggests bottle feeding and a formula. You are relieved that finally there is some kind of prescription, a method. No more of this improvisation. Already she will have to get used to a substitute. He hands you a piece of paper with the list of her injections and her height and length. Under "comments" he has written: Small, quiet, underdeveloped. Refuses breast. Skin irritations. Possible allergic reactions. You forget the paper on purpose in the waiting room. You do not need anything more in your house. And besides, it has become your habit to leave clues and traces of yourself behind, to make yourself easy to find.

Your home has taken a deep breath and expanded as things disappear into your dreams of whiteness. The radio has waves and bands that you do not understand, your chair was once a tree, so were your books, your papers, your letters. Photographs were only memories you tried to plan, develop, enlarge, but you don't know how. So they go. The dog is taking care of other things. A small twig chair which you thought you understood but now it is gone, a thin wooden woman someone sent you from Zimbabwe, a long strand of fertility shells, your father's pipe. You and the dog pass each other now and again as you put another thing in the give-away box, as the dog swallows something new. You each have your ways of getting rid of everything hard and corporeal. He takes it all into himself, enfolding these things into his big, hairy body, and you push everything away from you, thrusting. You gulp at each other, each creating more and more space for the other. The baby lies in her crib in the middle of your home staring up at the stained ceiling, while the world around her dismantles. Once she was tightly squeezed inside you, her palms pushing up against the walls of your body, of her galaxy, snug like a star embedded in a dark sky. Now all around her only air, and a looseness, something lax and adrift, everything collapsing around her each time she reaches out an uncontrolled fist to touch something. Sometimes when you leave the house, the dog sits staring out the window for a long time until in a panic he finds something else to destroy. You are beginning to see that there is a very fine line between solitude and confinement.

The dog eats through the wires of the telephone and holds the receiver between his paws like a bone. You bend down beside him and whisper into his big pointy ears: Hello? Hello? You make your voice and breath reverberate like an echo and he shakes his head from side to side. Sometimes when he is sitting straight and still, the tips of his paws a little flexed, his brown and yellow eyes narrowing, you let him stare at you and you hold his dark gaze, and in the quiet of this strange contest, you feel his wildness coming at you like advice and instinct. Do not move. Do not be moved.

In your search for something essential, your whole life has ended up in your cramped front yard. What here is blameless? Everything has been touched by you, objects hold the traces of all your vibrations, everywhere you've put your awful hands. You remember a story about a woman who decapitated two of her children right on her front lawn. Inside her house many more children shrugged their shoulders high over their ears. The days are still warm. Bicycles are chained to the iron fences all down your block. The days are still a little too long. The baby sits in her infant carrier on your cement stairs between an old pair of roller skates and a collection of Bee Gees albums. People come by and all make the same jokes. "How much for the baby?" Sometimes they answer their own jokes, strangers playing with each other, a regular amateur night right on your own front stoop. "The baby's free. Twenty bucks for the carrier." "Just kidding." They laugh and pun together, various snorts at different levels, and ride away happy in this friendly neighbourhood, on their old second-hand bicycles. Sometimes the women will give you an extra smile just to make sure you are taking it well. Some have heard of fluctuating hormones before. Really, you think of yourself as the carrier, the infant carrier going real cheap, the one who seems immune to disease but can surely pass it on.

It is not an official sale. Nothing is priced. Some things you give away for free, some you sell, depending on the person. That's the way that you are. At night you can hear people or animals picking at the things you've left on the curb. During the days, you wait and watch. The ones who spend the most time milling about seem to be artists of some kind. The girls tie scarves around their heads and wear jean overalls over printed cotton bras. They ask: Can we have this? Or this? You give them whatever they want. They pick up an old mirror frame, a scrap piece of paper, an old tassel lamp shade and turn it over and over in their wondrous hands. Everything they touch is "cool." You watch as they stuff your house into their deep canvas sacks. The dog hunches beside you, his head hangs low and saggy and the fur around his face and the tips of his paws is smeared an oily red from a tube of lipstick he ate just this morning. They walk away in their big-soled shoes with pieces of your life sticking out from the tops of their bags.

"Are you moving?" asks a neighbour, leaning over her second-floor balcony, looking down on you as you sit perfectly still on your cement stairs. It is such an incredible question that you are forced to take it apart, to dismantle it for its meaning. You feel hard and marbleized like a column or pillar. The baby is dirty and her skin is patchy and rough. You have let her nails grow into spiky rodent claws and she has scratched painful little animal tracks down her face. No. You are not moving. What you mean to say is that you haven't decided yet. Maybe if you give it

all away, free everything from your small home, jolt and prod all
these attachments until they fall loose like broken teeth. All
these things you've tried to eat, to make a part of you; all these
things you've touched and used, covered in your fingerprints,
dusty with the flakes of your own skin, if you could sweep all
this from you, maybe you would not be the one who had to
leave. You will be the one who stays, like the dog. You will not
be moved.

She is smeared with you. Her misshapen head, the small brown
birth mark on the inside of her thigh. She turned inside you,
somersaults and strange twists, and coated herself in you like
breaded chicken. Sometimes her arms seem like broken wings,
all their movements spastic and sore. How will she ever get
away from you like this? When you change her, you put her
down in the middle of your bare room, and there are moments
when you find your hands squeezed tight around her thin thighs.
You squeeze until you can touch the tip of your thumb to a
finger. You squeeze until you see a slight eruption in her face
that might mean she will cry. You drag your hands and fingers
across her small body, trying to leave clues. *I touched you here.
My nails dug here. Pieces of my skin settled on you like baby
powder. A slim strand of hair has fallen across your chest.*
    In the park where you go to sit alone sometimes, you have
seen women walking away from their children, screaming
something like "that's it" or "I've had enough." The children
fall to the ground and a cry moves so slowly through their body,
undulating in every part of them, you can see the thing right
below the surface of their skin, like fish rising suddenly to feed.
There is nothing but the end of the world and a woman walking
away. They stumble after their mothers, their arms stretched
forward like sleepwalkers, or Frankensteins. And the women
always turn back, always bend and open their arms, baring their
conspicuous chest, their heavy longing. You are the mammal
that is attracted to being the world to someone. A mother bear
chases her cub right up a tree, something she might have done
once in a time of danger, but this time she turns around and

leaves the cub behind. A bear knows what kind of animal she is. She walks away shaking her big head from side to side. This time, she is the danger.

For the last time you dress the baby in something yellow and terry cloth and picking her up off the floor you put her in her carrier and face her towards the door, perfectly lined up on the slats of polished wood, as though there were invisible tracks, like at the car wash, or some amusement-park ride. It is time, you think, and you are so sleepy that if you lay down here in your bare house you might never get up. Before she lies on her back and puts her foot in her mouth. Before she starts to recognize familiar faces. Before she ever mimics you, smiles when you smile, curls her wet soft lips when you do. You have to go now, you say to her. I'm no good. But she has closed her eyes and will not look at you. The dog waits on the floor, his head resting on his front legs stretched out ahead of him. He is still skinny, though much of your house is actually inside him. From the back, in her round summer cap and her reclining seat, the baby looks like a little astronaut, pointed towards the moon, waiting. You watch her, half expecting at any moment that she will be lifted from you in a great fire, leaving you behind, scorched and amazed, while she grows lighter and lighter, solemnly giving up gravity. Her cap blows away. Her bald head is a white milky planet, a round pearly moon.

Someone told you once that you were alive beyond your control. And each morning when you wake up you find that you are breathing before you even have a chance to try it another way. Just by sheer will you cannot stop your heart. On and on it goes like some boring aunt at a family gathering. On the day you carry your mother's black box and the blue rented telephone to the curb, the dog runs out into the street and is hit by the passing garbage truck. The garbage men bury their faces in their big orange gloves. You watch them from the top of your stairs. One of them leans over the animal and then quickly steps back, wiping his boots along the pavement as he does. They look around, expecting some kind of screaming at any moment. When they finally notice you, one of them steps forward and starts to come halfway up your walk. He takes off his orange glove and tucks it under his armpit. He is the one who hangs on from the back of the truck, one leg swinging back and forth, ready to jump at any moment. You shrug your shoulders and say: It wasn't mine. There is no one around to verify. Somehow you sense that he expects more from you, some kind of feminine shuddering that might mark the passing of a life. But you do nothing. Inside the truck you can see the driver crying. They decide to take the dog away. They take off their gloves and handle him with their bare hands. They flip his body into the truck and you can see that his head is leaning against a bag stuffed with leaves. You turn away and pretend not to hear the noise of the machine as it churns and pulls everything into itself making room for more.

Now that your house is empty, your dreams are suddenly crowded and smoky. In your dreams it happens this way: They surround your house and you raise your baby above your head in surrender, saying – I give up. I give up. The social worker steps forward and, rising on her petite tip-toes, takes her from you. In another one, you exchange her quickly in some alley like a drug deal. When she is gone you open your palm to find a round black metal ball. You swallow it, and every time you move you hear it rolling through you, tapping against your bones, ricocheting down your spinal cord, making you clang and echo with each step. You sign a paper waiving your parental rights and your hands surprise you by shaking, undulating like great white banners of surrender. You open and close your hand in front of your child's small folded face and ask for the last time: Can you wave bye bye, Baby? In your empty house you fully expect to sit here and make yourself disappear into a place where touch isn't possible, where nothing can come leaning up against you, or accidentally graze you from behind, where there's no kneading or fumbling or accidental impact. Do not move, you think. Don't make a sound. And with this advice it is unclear if you are prey or predator. What will happen? There are so many possibilities and the imagination is always unfaithful, adulterous and inexact with all its crazy footpaths anywhere. You wait in the middle of your living room, lying on the floor with your arms and legs spread out into an X, like a pale painted blotch on some forest tree, a clue someone left so that they could find their way back, something that marks a familiar spot.

K.D. MILLER

Egypt Land

Years after my father died, I dreamed that he was walking across a desert. His feet were in leather sandals, the ancient kind that loop around the big toe, weave across the instep, then strap around the ankle. In my dream, I could not take my eyes off my father's right foot.

I had never seen his right foot. I had never seen any part of his right leg, except the stump, peeking out of his swim trunks like a pink Parker House roll.

His artificial leg used to lean upright in a corner of my parents' bedroom when he didn't have it on. Its foot was smooth and featureless like a mannequin's foot, and its knee was bolted like the neck of Frankenstein's monster.

Yet here in my dream was a restored, fleshly leg. A perfectly ordinary right leg, knee poking through the fabric of my father's robe, thigh thrusting forward, keeping time with its left counterpart, walking through the sand.

Walking. In my dream, my dead father walked like everyone else. He didn't have to take a lurching step with his good leg, hitch the artificial one off the ground, swivel it forward, balance on it for half a second, then lurch onto the good leg again before the artificial knee could buckle under his weight. Kitchen floors and scatter rugs were treacherous for him in life. A single mile of sand like this would have exhausted him.

But he walked and walked, not at all tired by the heat or the ocean of sand. Sometimes he kicked the sand like spray. Sometimes he dug down with his feet and waded through it.

He smoked Export "A" unfiltered, leaving a trail of butts behind him that the wind buried as quickly as it buried his footprints. He lit each cigarette inside a little cave he made of his hands. Both his hands. For his left hand had been restored too, like his right leg.

A stroke had paralysed his left side when he was sixty. His left hand lay in his lap for ten years until he died. It had to be lifted and poked into the sleeve of a shirt. It could wear a mitt but not a glove, for the fingers were frozen into a half-formed fist.

But now it waved a flame into smoke and flicked the blackened match away onto the sand. Then it reached down to adjust the rope sash that kept the robe lapped over his stomach. At last it strayed to his crotch and scratched there gently.

I waited for my mother's hissed, "Bill! Stop that!" Subconsciously, I was expecting her to keep trying to neaten and tidy him and make him nice, even after his death. But my mother was not in the dream. Neither was I. Not yet. My father walked the desert alone.

Except for the camel.

In my father's right hand was a leather rein that he transferred to the crook of his elbow whenever he was lighting a cigarette. The rein led to a leather bridle which the camel wore as it walked along behind my father, swaying like a big ambulatory plant. On either side of its hump was a tarp-covered load, professionally tied up, expertly strapped on.

Everything in my dream had that air about it that dreamed things do, of making perfect sense on their own terms. So no doubt my restored father would have loaded the back of the camel as matter-of-factly as he used to load the back of his pickup. "Yeah, yeah, *tell* me about it," he would have said around a cigarette when the animal groaned in token protest.

When they stopped at last for a rest, the camel lowered its belly to the sand, first its front end, then its back. My father sat down in the shadow it cast. He pulled off his burnoose, scrunched it like a baseball cap, swabbed his face and neck with it, then put it back on. He was clean-shaven, as in life, and his white hair was still brush-cut. His eyes were the ice blue I remembered, the pupils small dots of perfect black.

He looked out over the sand with a look I recognized. It was a look that saw what it saw, and knew what it knew. His eyes shifted often and blinked seldom. I remember him looking that way at the surface of water. He would stand on his one leg on a beach, shoulders pushed high by his crutches, studying the lake as if his gaze could pierce its moving surface. He would hump-swing several yards into the water, throw his crutches like spears back onto shore, then dive. Once in the water, he was as free as a seal.

So I knew this look. And I recognized the way he now puckered his lips, and I heard before hearing it the cool thready whistle he breathed out. A single note, perhaps two. A phrase of a song known only to him. Long silences between notes. Then, after the longest silence, perhaps a lyric or two, more spoken than sung. Sometimes enough to allow the song to be identified. "Flow Gently, Sweet Afton," or "The Surrey with the Fringe on Top," or "Red Sails in the Sunset."

The broken music-making ended at last, before the sun had quite set. In the colouring light, my father reached into a fold of his robe and brought forth the yellow vendor's copy of a purchase order. The carbon type was blurred, but legible.

"Go down, Moses," the purchase order sang as soon as it was unfolded, "Way down to Egypt land. Tell old Pharaoh to let my people go."

My father folded it back up, and abruptly the singing stopped.

"Sure," he muttered around a cigarette, the last before sleep. "You betcha." He waved the flame into smoke. "You just betcha." He flicked the match away. Though his eyes followed its flight, in the growing darkness he could not see where it landed.

Egypt Land. The idea of Egypt. The thought of it. Even the word. The dream brought it all back.

"Eee-jipt," I used to whisper to myself, hands cupped over ears to catch my own voice. "Eee-jipt." It was the most alien-sounding, most mysterious word I knew.

I felt responsible for Egypt. Knowing that the Sphinx's face was almost worn away by time, the pyramids long emptied by adventurers and thieves, threw me into a kind of panic. I hated to think of the treasures scattered over the world, some trapped in glass cases, others traded and sold, changing hands until no one remembered what they really were. I tortured myself with crazy thoughts of Nefertiti's necklace lost in the beady clutter on top of my mother's dresser. Or, in a dark corner of my father's workbench, behind a jar of wing nuts, the golden mask of a god, jewelled eyes serene, patiently waiting to be worshipped again.

I wanted so much to find the lost treasures and return them to Egypt. I ached to restore the face of the Sphinx.

"Can't they pick up the pieces that have fallen off and stick them back on with something?" My mother always said my father could fix anything.

"Nope. The wind's worn them away. They're spread all over the place."

"But are they still *there?* Couldn't somebody find them and pick them up?"

"They're too small to recognize. They just look like sand."

I would recognize them. I would know them from sand. "But are they *somewhere?* Do they –" I didn't know the word I wanted.

"Exist? Oh yeah. I guess so. Nothing ever stops existing."

How could he know that the Sphinx's nose might be lying around in plain sight, albeit changed, and feel no need to do something about it?

I needed to save Egypt Land. I needed to find every particle of it, however tiny, and put it back in its place. I saw myself travelling all over the world, all my life, asking questions, following leads, finding, taking, breaking into museums, haunting white-elephant sales, stealing, liberating, restoring.

If I could bring all the pieces back together, I could bring Egypt Land back to life. I could point the edges of the pyramids, curl the lip of the Sphinx. I could make the wind carry the smell of incense and sweet oils, the sound of pipes and drums. And through the very heart of Egypt Land, I could make Pharaoh walk again.

It was my father who told me about Egypt in the first place. He gave the impression of having discovered Egypt all by himself long ago, long before me, long before my mother, before his leg came off, before he was even born. There was something ageless about my father, like the burnoose and sandals and camel he was equipped with in my dream. Hymn-book phrases like "the Ancient of Days" used to make me think of him.

"Akhenaton wasn't your run-of-the-mill Pharaoh," I remember him telling me. "For one thing, he'd made up his mind that there was only one God, instead of half a dozen or so, and that he himself wasn't it. That made him pretty damned strange for an Egyptian, and even stranger for a Pharaoh. That's how come he tacked 'aton' onto his name. It was the name of his God. Then along came Tut, and monotheism went to hell."

Tutankhamen's tomb had been discovered early in my father's childhood. His whole growing-up world had been coloured by the Egyptomania raging for years after the discovery.

"Chances are, if Akhenaton had lived longer, just to give Tut a chance to grow up some, and learn something from him, Egypt might of been a different place. And all kinds of things around it and coming after it might of been different too."

My father had once been a reader. I used to find his books in the house and put them on my own bookshelf in my bedroom. *Moby Dick*, *Morte d'Arthur*, *The Odyssey*. Books he read before his leg came off and he had to quit school. The print was archaic, the pages faintly browned at the edges. They smelled of dust and damp rags. On the inside front cover of each, in ink-bottle ink, was my father's name, school and classroom number. I tried to imagine him in a cap and plus-fours, but couldn't. And all he ever read now was the sports section and the comics.

But he did once read about Egypt and the Pharaohs, the way he read about everything else. Voraciously until the age of fourteen, then not at all.

So what was he doing as Moses, Pharaoh's archenemy, in my dream?

When I was in Sunday School, I had a problem with Moses, for all that he was the good guy and Pharaoh the bad. I thought Moses had an unfair advantage, namely God.

"God hardened Pharaoh's heart," Miss Urquhart would gasp

at us in the basement of the church. "He hardened his heart so he wouldn't let the Israelites go, not even when the plague of frogs came. Just imagine, children! A plague of frogs! Frogs hopping all over your plate at supper! Frogs hopping across your bed at night!"

Well, we thought a plague of frogs would be kind of neat, and besides we liked the way Miss Urquhart's face dropped like a stone whenever we laughed at stuff she thought was serious. Miss Urquhart had the most unfortunate of Scots Presbyterian facial types, nose meeting chin, tiny lashless eyes close together. So we laughed and her face dropped and God hardened our hearts and we laughed some more.

Miss Urquhart illustrated her stories with paper cut-outs which she stuck onto a green felt board where they sometimes, miraculously, stayed. There was Moses, facing right, marching across the board to Egypt Land. There, in the middle, were the enslaved Israelites, all in a cut-out mass, crayoned brown. And there, aloof on the far right, was Pharaoh.

Actually, he was a pen-and-ink sketch of Tutankhamen's sarcophagus, but I didn't know that then. All I knew was that Pharaoh was beautiful. He was serene. He stared straight ahead, straight out from the green felt board, unmoved by the fuss being made by Moses and the Israelites and God and Miss Urquhart.

As an adult I finally saw the real Tutankhamen. That is, I saw his sarcophagal mask, through glass, from behind a velvet rope.

I wanted to touch his lips. Ridiculous thing to want to do, I knew, because Tutankhamen's lips had been made about as untouchable as anything could be. The whole Treasures of the Tomb exhibit was policed by uniformed guards who shouted, "Please do not touch the glass! Please keep your hands away from the glass!" every thirty seconds.

Maybe they had to do that because everybody felt the way I did about touching that smooth gold cheek, that sweet mouth. There is an irresistible boyish eagerness to Tutankhamen's face. For all its stillness and formality, there is something anticipatory in the expression. A kind of hope.

I have no pictures of my father as a boy. What that means, among other things, is that I have never seen even so much as a picture of his right leg.

When he was fourteen, he went picking berries. He spent the whole day on his knees, and when he tried to get up he could not straighten out his right leg. The next morning, he still could not straighten it out, and it had gone pure white, except for the faintest trace of green.

My father did not talk about losing his leg. He told my mother the story exactly once, and she told it to me several times. A grim comedy of errors led to the amputation, a combination of ignorance and complacency that favoured folk remedies, salt baths and a good night's sleep over calling a doctor. By the time a doctor was reluctantly called, my father's toes had turned black.

His leg came off in stages as the gangrene advanced. First the foot, then the ankle, then the calf just below the knee, then the knee, then most of the thigh. The procedure took an entire year, during which time he did not leave the hospital. When he finally got out on crutches, the whole world had become the Depression. There was no more school for him, and no more reading.

Though I am able to imagine my father with a young face, there is an expression I cannot make it assume. The features have a basic rigidity in my memory, and they resist all my attempts to mould them.

The nurses kept him busy during that year in the hospital. Occupational therapy was still a thing of the future, but they taught him what they knew, knitting, rug-hooking, even embroidery. I have a baby dress that he trimmed in pink embroidery thread. One night, when my mother simply forgot how to do blanket stitch, he remembered.

But the nurses could not do anything about what was happening to his face. And neither can I now. I cannot remove from it the mask of resignation.

I'm told that nobody is ever miscast in a dream. But Moses? Moses the rebel? Moses the justice-seeker?

In the wake of my dream I reread the Book of Exodus. It seems that Moses was an unwilling liberator of the Israelites. He had been raised in the Egyptian royal household, after all, and Pharaoh was his adopted grandfather. So he protested to God that he couldn't possibly tell the old man to let the Israelites go because he was no good at public speaking. God got around that one by letting him take along his brother Aaron, who apparently had the gift of the gab.

Maybe that was why my father was restored in my dream. Maybe he protested to the issuer of the purchase order that he couldn't walk the desert with an artificial right leg, a paralysed left leg and a paralysed left arm. That he couldn't do it as the head, hand and torso he had become.

"Don't keep busted tools hanging around!"

It was summer, and I was sitting on the bottom basement step to read, because that was the coolest spot in the house. My father was at his workbench with his back to me when he said that about tools. He was lit by one hanging yellow bulb, his undershirt a white Y against his freckled back. He worked while he spoke, his arms reaching out to right and left. Bolts and hinges and screws. Bits and pieces, each, however small or dusty, compartmentalized in a dirty cardboard box according to specific use. Jars filled with nails in exact gradations. The smells of metal and sawdust. Paint, turpentine, varnish and oil.

"A busted tool is a piece of junk!"

He respected tools. He would tinker and mutter lovingly for hours over a broken tool. If it could be fixed. If it could not, he would throw it away without a moment's sentiment or regret. It was the usefulness of tools he liked, their capacity for work. There was an air of rarefied contentment about him when he was doing a job. I recognized this in my dream. I saw it in the flare of his lit match, the creases of his knuckles, the still line of his mouth. He hadn't chosen to go down to Egypt Land, but it was a job. Work was work.

I never knew when he was going to come out with one of these life-lessons. We could be together for hours, he puttering,

I reading, without a single word being exchanged. Then all at once he would speak. It was as if he had suddenly remembered I was his child, and perhaps in need of wisdom.

"There're guys I know, haven't got the brains they were born with when it comes to busted tools. And their shops are full of junk. You ever get yourself something that won't work, don't fart around with it. Fix it or chuck it out."

He lived for ten years after the stroke paralysed him. I only heard him protest once.

It was just a few weeks after it happened. My mother and I had been visiting him at night, and she was getting him settled down in his hospital bed. His left arm and leg had to be bolstered with pillows to keep him from rolling on them in the night. While she was doing that, I stepped out into the hall to give them some time alone.

The second I was out of sight, my father's voice rose in a long, cantorial wail. Wordless, higher and higher, thinner and thinner, it followed me down the hall into the elevator, found me even in the lobby, where I tried to hide from it.

The degree of my father's brokenness, the thing his life had become, terrified me. Any slip of the mask, any crack in his resignation, was an occasion for panic.

But the occasions were few. I never in fact heard him cry again. In time, the professionals deemed him "completely adjusted" to his situation.

Maybe he was. Or maybe the Continuing Care wing wasn't as awful as I remember it.

It did have a disturbing smell. Not a bad smell, for it was kept very clean. The smell was delicate enough, but cloying. It was the smell of human flesh. Bathed and powdered. Animate. But inert.

Every morning of the ten years he was there, my father lay sandbagged by pillows, waiting for a nurse to come. The nurse would check the urine bag hanging out from under the bedclothes, then syringe the catheter tube that went up his penis into his bladder, to see if it was still drawing. She and another nurse would dress my father, pull him into a sitting position and slide him along a board into his wheelchair. There he would sit all day until it was time for him to go to bed again.

He lived in a room with three other men. One of these lay perpetually asleep on his back, eyelids purple, nose and chin jutting up from a sunken mouth that sucked and blew like an oyster hole. He finally died and was replaced by another sleeping man, whose sleep was like waves, rolling and mumbling.

My father was born down near the bay, in the east end of Hamilton. He swam in the bay when he was a boy, and worked there as a lifeguard when he was in his twenties. There is a photograph of him sitting up high on a lifeguard's lookout chair, staring out at the water with that look he gave the desert sand in my dream.

I asked him once how he could be a one-legged lifeguard, and he said that if he spotted anybody in trouble, he would hop down off his perch, grab his crutches, run on them to the water's edge, then dive. "I had three legs to the other guys' two," he said. "I could go like a spider."

He pointed his old neighbourhood out to me once while we stood on the edge of the Hamilton escarpment. This is a rise of three hundred feet or so, just enough to make the lower city look small and old. Down there, he had been born into established poverty. My mother had been born on the "mountain" into new wealth.

Two or three times a year, my father would come up the stairs to my room to tell me stories of the east end. I would hear his slow step, his good leg pulling the artificial one up, the clump of the wooden foot, then another step, then another pull. And I would hear my mother calling, "Bill! She has homework to do!"

He would come into my room without saying anything to me, sometimes without looking at me. He would sit down heavily in my dresser chair and examine the walls for cracks, the ceiling for stains, the floor tiles for upraised corners. "Got to fix that," he would mutter when he spotted something.

Or his eye might lock onto something of mine, a pyramid of bristly curlers on my dresser, or a pink plastic hand whose splayed fingers were to hold rings. He would stare at it silently for several seconds. Then he would pick it up, turning it quarter-inch by quarter-inch, perhaps taking it apart and putting it back together. I never told him what these things were for. His investigation lent them a dignity far above the actual. To reveal that they were for curling hair or displaying baubles would somehow have disappointed him.

And he was a disappointed enough man. He never talked about it, but I sensed his disappointment, as I might sense the lip of a hole just beyond my feet in the dark.

After a silence, he would light the first cigarette and begin, "You know, when I was a boy down in the east end . . ."

Aside from that bird's-eye view of his old neighbourhood from the escarpment, I had never seen the east end. It was as huge and as vague in my imagination as Troy or Xanadu. If I had ever been driven through it, I probably would have been shocked by the absence of horses clopping by, bobbing their heads in rhythm with their feet, like clumsy dancers.

It wasn't sentiment or nostalgia that brought my father to my room, though all his stories were of his first fourteen years. There was more a feeling of necessity about the telling, even of inevitability, as if something had finally come to the surface, something buried for centuries, that might explode in the air.

So I knew enough to listen silently as he told me about a woman whose self-appointed task was to gather old woollens from all the households in the neighbourhood, then unravel, dye and retwist the yarn. She would give it back to each mother according to need, so that the neighbourhood children would have warm clothes. "One winter, we was all outfitted in green. The next year, kind of a tangerine colour. Depended on whatever dyestuffs she happened to have lyin' around. Nobody paid her. Nobody could of paid her. She just done it."

Throughout the telling, my mother would listen loudly downstairs, sometimes rattling her newspaper, once or twice calling up that it was a school night, and that I had to get to bed soon.

My father hardly responded to her protests. His mouth might twist, or he might stub a cigarette out a little harder than usual, using the silver paper from the pack as an ad hoc ashtray.

I didn't want him to come to my room. I didn't want him not

to. He was there. Talking for once, the way he almost never talked. So I listened.

Maybe he had once talked to my mother that way. Maybe she had once listened, silently, uncritically, the way I did. I felt sorry for her. But I felt proud of myself.

He would talk for half an hour or so, punctuating the talk with long silences. He hissed smoke out from between his teeth during these, staring straight ahead, snagged on a memory.

I listened on through the silences. I didn't question or probe or dig, but let the thing emerge as it would. I heard his diction and his grammar slipping farther back into the east end, and just let them. And when the story was finished, I let the sound of it hang in the air like the smoke of his cigarette.

"Me an' Ernie . . ." he began once, speaking of a boyhood chum who disappeared from his life about the time he lost his leg. "We used t'go around together, an' the other kids used t'step out of the way when they seen us comin'. 'Cause anybody pick on one of us, he'd hafta deal with the other one too. We was fighters, Ernie an' me. We was on our way to being real street fighters. Kids used t'talk about the day me an' Ernie would fight each other. They used t'wait for it, like they'd wait for the day of a prize fight. But that day never come."

He had no friends that I knew of. He went to work. He came home. I used to look at him and wonder if he loved my mother and me. If he loved anyone. Then I would try to love him, try to feel myself loving him. Maybe, I thought, there was something wrong with the way I was doing it. Maybe, if I really loved him, I would dig and dig at him the way my mother did. And his silence, his aloofness, would chafe me the way it did her.

"I shopped today, Bill," she would try over supper, watching him while he ate. "And I washed and ironed." She would continue to watch, and he to eat. "I got my hair done, too!" At last she would grab up her plate and clatter it into the sink. "Not a word!" she would call to the air. "No answer!"

If he said anything at all, it would be, "You didn't ask a question, did you?"

I knew it must have been different between them once. He

had, after all, climbed the mountain, courted and won her. She had been engaged to another man, the kind she had been raised for, but had broken it off when she met Bill. I've seen a picture of them on their honeymoon. She's sitting on his lap and their faces look as if they're hurting with smiles.

But at some point, for some reason, he stopped even trying to speak the language of the mountain. At the same time, she stopped even trying to tolerate the language of the east end.

"So I goes down to the shop –"

"I *go* down to the shop."

"And I says –"

"And I *say*."

"I says, look fella, you gonna get off the pot an' close this deal or ain'tcha?"

The two of them might as well have inhabited different countries. My mother was a pretty woman, a fussy woman, uncomfortable with dirt and noise and vulgarity. Her country was the house, from the laundry tubs in the basement, up through the kitchen, into the farthest corners of the linen closet and up into my room, where she poked under my bed with her mop, dragging out grey tumbleweeds of dust.

Her country's boundaries extended out into the back yard, where she talked over the fence with Mrs. Kiraja. Each woman stood with her laundry basket balanced on one hip, sometimes dabbing at the front of her hair in a token tidying gesture. They called each other "Mrs." and spoke in hushed, courteous tones, looking directly into each other's wide eyes. Though they might shift their laundry baskets from one hip to the other, they would never put them down on the ground, for to do this would be to imply that they actually had the time to talk.

"A man he works from sun to sun," my mother would sometimes recite, "But a woman's work is never done." She liked poems that rhymed, and she liked hymns, the older and more syrupy the better. Sometimes, in the middle of the day, in her housedress, with dust motes boiling up from the keys, she would play the piano and sing, "And He *walks* with me and He *talks* with me, and He tells me I am his *own* . . ." Or

"Jerusalem," or "The Old Rugged Cross," or "Onward Christian Soldiers," all in her girlish soprano.

She came into her own on Sunday. She was the chooser of shirts, the straightener of ties, the whitener of shoes and the mender of gloves. In church, she bloomed while my father looked artificial.

My father's country, his world of work, was roughly male, utterly without ornament. He drove into gravelled lots behind machine shops. He hollered to men above the scream of machinery, and they yelled back.

I doubt that my mother ever went on a day-long sales trip with my father the way I sometimes did. I couldn't imagine her doing such a thing, or him asking her to.

I never knew what prompted him to ask me. The places we visited were identical islands of noise dotting long, silent miles of highway. Dusty offices flimsily attached to dustier shops. Screen doors that banged. Plants quietly browning in curtainless windows. Chipped arborite counters with men behind them whose eyes widened when they saw my father, and who called him "Bill!"

My father pushed his hat to the back of his head in these places, and leaned his elbows on the counter, his hips cocked at an angle. He talked loud, saying "this here" and "not nothin'." His grin was fixed and fierce. He barked a laugh that would have made my mother look away and sniff.

"Got my sweetie with me!" he would say to explain my presence. Or, "This here's my honey!" I would stare warm-faced at the floor while roars of "Hey, hey, hey!" and "Ain't she a cutie!" crashed like waves over my head.

Then a great to-do would be made about what was to be done with me, where I was to be put, while business was conducted. "She can sit right over there! Yeah! She'll be fine, won'tcha, Honey?" One of the behind-the-counter men once found me a dusty, cellophane-wrapped sucker.

Sometimes I was allowed to explore the concrete interiors of shops, the piled industrial barrels full of hardware. The floors of these places were dotted with pools of oil. The only natural light pushed through the grime of small, high windows. This was the world of my father's work. And I, for some reason, was being shown that world.

I didn't like going on those trips. They were boring, and the day felt long. My father was not good company. I had trouble thinking of anything to say to him as we drove along between shops, and whatever I did say was usually met with silence.

The silence was something that came from him, just as his stories came from him. It had the same feeling of necessity, of inevitability. So I let it be, and waited for him to break it. And when he didn't, I looked out the window and counted cows.

It felt like a mission. A duty. A role. To be there. To listen. To receive whatever parts of himself he chose to give.

I tried not to think about my mother home all day alone. It felt like a betrayal, leaving her behind. But staying with her would have felt like betraying my father.

I still sometimes wonder if my father stopped speaking her language once I was born, once I began to hear, and see, and remember.

My father seldom touched me. I remember him holding me only once. It was when I was very small, and was trying to teach him to run.

"See? Watch me! You run like this!" I ran around him in a circle. "And you jump like this!" I jumped and landed and fell over backwards. I got up and tugged at his belt. "Come on and run!" I begged. "Come on! I'll show you!"

He caught the back of my head and pressed my face into his stomach. He smelled of tobacco and sweat. Be still, the hand on my head said. Be silent, said the mingled scents.

"Oh, look what she's brought, Bill! Bill, look!"

We were sitting at a table in the Continuing Care coffee shop. We spent a lot of time there during visits to my father because it was one of the few spots that still allowed smoking.

"Oh, *look*, Bill!" My mother was turning the pages of the glossy *Treasures of the Tomb* catalogue I had bought at the

Royal Ontario Museum. She was leaning in towards my father so that he could see too.

"It's an incredible exhibit, Dad," I said in the sitcom daughter-chirp I had adopted since his stroke. "Really worth seeing." I had also mentally installed an automatic editor that kept me from saying things like "You should go and see it." It was all part of the enforced good cheer that got me through these visits. I came once a month, armed with conversation pieces.

"Bill? *Look* at it, for heaven's sake! You should *look* at this when she's taken the trouble to bring it all the way from Toronto! Look at the mask, Bill!"

He did look at the mask of Tutankhamen, and I wondered, fearfully, what he might be remembering. I imagined telling him about wanting to put my hand through the glass and touch those golden lips, about how moved I was by the expression on the face of the boy-king. But the automatic editor hardened my heart, and I was silent.

"They were a cruel people, the Egyptians," my mother said, turning the page. "They kept slaves and made them pull big rocks up the sides of the pyramids." She turned another page to a photograph of a life-sized golden cobra. "Ugh!" she said, and turned again.

The cobra had been one of my favourite parts of the exhibit. I had stood in front of its glass case for ages, understanding how such a thing might be worshipped.

All at once my father said, "They wasn't slaves, most of them." We both looked at him.

"Yes, they *were*," my mother said. I almost raised a hand to silence her. "And they had to pull big rocks –"

"Most of 'em was indentured servants. They worked for so many years, then they could go anywhere they liked. Most of 'em stayed in Egypt. 'Cause they liked it there."

I hadn't heard him talk, really talk, for ages. Since the stroke his talk had been mostly monosyllabic answers to my mother's questions. Was he too hot, was he too cold, would he like some more coffee, did he want to play Scrabble again?

My mother had become a Continuing Care volunteer in a

pink smock with a nametag. She visited my father every day. She checked his laundry, filled out his menu plan, printed his name on every page of his newspaper, went with him on outings and special events.

I went along with them to only one of those, a barbecue that got rained out and ended up as a singsong in the hospital auditorium. Patients of every age and condition were wheeled into a circle and given a songbook. One of the requests was for "Amazing Grace." They sang it, those who were not catatonic, those who could focus their eyes, those who could form words. The hymn rose in a great ragged moan while I stood there, pressing my back flatter and flatter against the wall. I could not decently escape, though something in the back of my mind was shrieking at me to run.

For there, hunched in his wheelchair, head bent, eyes following my mother's pointing finger, was my father. Singing ". . . once was lost, but now am found . . ."

"What about the Israelites?" I said now. I wanted to keep him talking. "What's the Book of Exodus all about if they weren't enslaved by the Egyptians?"

"The Israelites were originally under contract to make bricks. There was nothin' like slavery going on. Not for generations, anyway. They had no land and they had nothin' to eat, so they settled down in Egypt and went to work for Pharaoh. Simple as that." He stubbed out his cigarette and began picking the cellophane off a fresh pack.

"Don't open that," my mother said. "You've smoked enough."

My father ignored her. He would not speak again until his new cigarette was lit, and he would not accept help getting it out of the pack.

It was quite an operation, getting and lighting a cigarette with one hand. First he had to pick a hole in the cellophane, peel it off, open the lid of the pack and pull away the silver paper. Then he had to inch one cigarette out, using thumb and index finger, anchoring the pack on the table with the heel of his palm. It was the first thing he had learned in occupational therapy, and the first indication to the professionals that he was "accepting" and "adjusting."

"You'll see," my mother said, watching him. "They're going to make this a no-smoking area too."

"Then I'll go outside."

"It's *cold* outside."

"Then I'll freeze my butt."

"Bill!"

"What about Moses?" I said quickly.

"What about him?"

"Why did he have such a tough time getting the Israelites out of Egypt, if nothing was holding them there?"

"Oh, by then somethin' was. They *was* slaves by the time Moses come along."

"*Came* along. See? I said they were slaves. They had to pull big rocks up the sides of the –"

"Who made them slaves?" Couldn't she see that something was happening? That something was actually making the time move for a change?

"Pharaoh made 'em slaves. One of the last big Pharaohs. Just before everything started goin' to hell."

"Bill, you don't have to shout." My mother cut her eyes around the coffee shop, convinced as always that the chatting nurses and dozing patients were hanging on our every word.

"See, by the time Moses come along, Egypt was bein' chipped away at by everybody an' his brother. The Middle East was the same mess it is today." There was a small spot of pink on each of my father's cheeks. His right fist was clenched. "So Pharaoh hunkered down an' tried to hang on to what he had. An' what he had was this great big bunch of Hebes –"

"Bill!"

"– who'd been multiplying like hell for generations an' were as unified as all-get-out with their one God. He got scared they might side with his enemies an' attack him from the inside. So he done somethin' real dumb. Instead of makin' them his allies, he made them his slaves. Tried to work 'em to death."

"And that was King Tut who did that, was it?" my mother

said in the wrap-up tone she used to use for "and they all lived happily ever after."

"Nope. By Moses' time Tut had been dead a hundred years."

"Well then, what's so special about King Tut, for heaven's sake?" She was frowning at the price sticker on the catalogue.

My father said nothing. He was looking off into middle distance with the look I would see again in my dream.

"Didn't Tutankhamen stamp out the monotheism that had just been introduced into Egypt?" I prompted.

He still said nothing. His cheeks were pale again, almost transparent. In the past weeks he had gotten very thin. The veins on his forehead could be seen to throb. And now he had simply stopped talking. As abruptly as he'd begun.

"Didn't that make Tut the most influential fifteen-year-old in history?" I was starting to sweat. It was *there*, damn it. I knew it was still there, if I could only dig down far enough. I could remember him spinning a whole alternative history of Egypt for me that started with Tutankhamen nurturing the radical new idea of one God, and ended with Moses and Pharaoh seeing eye to eye. No slavery, no bulrushes, no Exodus.

"Dad –?"

My mother put her hand on my forearm. Don't, her lips said. Don't. He can't.

I pulled my arm away. I hated her new solicitude, her regained powers. She would phone me sometimes and list all the things my father had been through in his life, and go on about what a shame it was, and how he'd done nothing to deserve any of it. I could hardly stand to listen, and I was jealous of her ability to say the words.

He was hers now. That time that he cried, she stayed in the room and I ran. She could look at his weakness. I needed to see him strong.

Sometimes I entertained a mad fantasy of renting a van, getting him into it somehow and taking him to a Canadian Tire store. Just so he could see something besides pastel uniforms and smell something besides talcum powder.

Maybe I could wheel him up and down the aisles, opening boxes for him. Letting him see again the precise gradations of nails and screws, feel again the oily smoothness of a brand new wrench. Or better still, maybe I could stay at the front near the cashiers and let him cruise the aisles alone.

I could see him pushing himself along in his wheelchair, stopping dead when something caught his eye. I could see him picking up whatever it was and cradling it for a moment in his palm, testing its weight. Then looking at its underside, its top, and each end in turn. At last laying it flat on his palm and bringing it level with his eye. Peering down its length. Checking it for straightness. For balance.

My father stubbed out his cigarette and reached for another one.

"Bill, that's your sixth since we've been sitting here!"

"Seventh," he said, flicking his lighter.

I did not properly mourn my father's death. In time I worried that this neglected mourning might have form, might be a *thing* inside me that would surface someday, the way buried stones and relics will frost-heave to the surface of the earth.

My first reaction to his death was to wonder, perhaps absurdly, perhaps not, where he was. Where he had gone.

A Continuing Care nurse had phoned my mother to tell her he was "going." My mother took a taxi to the hospital. She was able to piece together later that all the time she was in the taxi, my father was "going" but still "there." He was still "there" when she crossed the hospital lobby and stepped into the elevator. But when the elevator doors opened onto my father's floor, she was met by the nurse who had phoned her. "He's gone," the nurse said. "Just now."

So where did he go? I could not believe that he was nowhere, that he had simply stopped existing. Nothing ever stopped existing.

But I had never known him whole. A piece of him had always been missing. Over time, more and more pieces had gone missing. Over time, his words had become fewer, his silences longer. And now, here was this complete silence that might or might not be complete. I might or might not see and hear my father again.

He himself did have a God. That much I was sure of. It is

possible that as a boy he prayed for the gangrene to halt its advance, or at least to spare him his knee. It is possible that as an old man he prayed for his left arm and leg to come back to life. And it is possible that when both prayers went unanswered, he prayed to die.

Oh tell of His might, oh sing of His grace,
Whose robe is the light, whose canopy space . . .

The memorial service took place outside, on the edge of the escarpment. All through it, my mother held a small white cardboard box. I tried not to look at the box, but it drew my eye.

She had phoned me the night before, worried about the service, worried about whether the hymn she had picked out really had been my father's favourite, worried about which dress she should wear, worried about whether she should continue as a Continuing Care volunteer. She would stop and cry for a while into the phone, then blow her nose and start up again.

I let her chorus on, saying nothing. I had not, and would not for years, shed a tear. Tears would have been a comfort, and I did not deserve comfort.

"They were very nice to me, the people at the crematorium," she said into the phone. Then she hesitated. Her voice became small, the voice of a child confessing.

"They put it – you know – all in a nice white box. Very clean."

No, I thought. Surely not.

"It's – the ashes – I opened the box – the ashes are white. All white, like talcum powder. Except –"

No. I could not believe what I knew I was going to hear.

"– except they don't *feel* like talcum powder. They feel like sand."

At the end of the service she held the box out to me. I shook my head. How could I scatter him, disperse him, let him be more lost than he was?

She could. And when she had emptied the box, she held it for a moment upside down and tapped it gently.

There was a wind. Hating my own sentimentality, I imagined it blowing some of the ashes towards the east end.

His chariots of wrath the deep thunderclouds form,
And dark is His path on the wings of the storm.

My father's God was the God who said to Moses, "I shall be
gracious to whom I shall be gracious, and I shall have compassion on whom I shall have compassion." He was the God who
hardened Pharaoh's heart for the express purpose of making
things difficult.

My father knew this God in my dream, knew him long before
my dream. Had heard his muttering and felt his tinkering from
the age of fourteen.

"Come on now. Get down from there." I knew in my dream that
I wasn't really in trouble, even though my father had been called
out of death, as out of retirement, to come all the way to Egypt
Land to let me go.

"I said get down," he repeated. He hardly ever told me to do
anything. It felt strange when he did, like falling out of bed. But
even then I knew he wasn't really mad. He sounded as if he'd
caught me doing something more dumb than bad, and just didn't
want to make an issue of it.

He was standing at the bottom of the dais, looking up at me.
The camel peered over his shoulder. When it caught my eye, it
groaned its token protest at me, as if it thought I might unpack
its load.

I swung my feet for a little while longer. Pharaoh's throne was
a high one. I had to stretch my arms straight out to reach the
golden handrests. I was tired of playing Pharaoh, but it was hard
to stop. Somebody had to tell me to.

Finally, when I figured my father might be getting mad for
real, I slid down and landed with a thump. Then I came down the
steps of the dais slowly, dawdling on each one.

"Go on home to your mother now," he said. "Nothin' keeping you here." I dawdled some more, crouching and combing my
fingers through the sand. "I said go home!"

I asked him if I could keep the camel. He told me to go ask my
mother. Then he pointed to the load. "Tell her there's some
stuff in there," he said. "Stuff that's hers. I've been meaning to

let her have it." I knew without being told that I wasn't supposed to peek inside.

So I started for home, leading the camel by the rein. I watched myself walk out of the dream. I was very small, and quite brown. My footsteps filled with sand the second I made them. The camel walked behind me, lilypad feet splayed, laden hump swaying out of sync with belly.

Once I was over a sand dune and out of sight, my father went up the steps to Pharaoh's throne. He picked up Pharaoh's sceptre, which was leaning beside it. He hefted it in his palm, balanced it on his index finger, hoisted it to his shoulder and squinted down its length. So preoccupied, he sat down.

He became Old Pharaoh, and the Sphinx and the pyramids. He became the wind and the sand and the pipes and the drums and the incense and the sweet oils. He became Egypt Land.

MURRAY LOGAN

Steam

I'm getting to be the age where I no longer know the price of anything. Let me give you an example. I'm out with some woman or other. We stop for tea and blueberry scones and before the bill is totalled up I have five dollars ready. More than enough, you'd think, including a good tip. Then the machine flashes $5.24 and I'm left to fumble around, searching for a loose quarter. And the woman I'm with, girl really, young enough to be my daughter if you fudge a year here or there, is watching me. A black leather mini, ankle-socks trimmed with lace, little black fuck-me shoes, watching me search for a quarter. And afterward, of course, she wants to go drinking and dancing. And after that she'll want to come to my place, and I'll say we go to hers. I finish my tea, but she doesn't touch hers, I don't think she knows what it is, and I tell her I have a headache. I give her $40 for a cab or whatever and watch her walk away, black mini, one of those billowing $600 yellow leather jackets, long legs and all. Things change.

I go to a steam-bath near my place. It's in a community centre, you know, on the up and up. Just so you don't get the wrong idea. Like a sauna but better. I go, and I sit in that steam, and I come out refreshed, at peace. It's quite remarkable.

I don't go all the time, you understand, I don't like to be predictable. I don't like people to know who I am, where I'll be. Maybe I'll tell you why sometime.

The steam-bath, it's like a sauna. Wood. Benches. Fat guys

sweating. The door's different, though. A sauna, it has a wooden door. The steam-bath, it has a steel door, like an industrial fridge. To keep the steam in. There's a doohickey on the wall you pull, a valve, and more steam comes out. In a sauna what you do is sit there until you're bored of watching sweat drip off the end of your nose. In the steam bath, you sit there until you think you're going to die. Then you sit some more. When I leave, after having a long cold shower, sometimes I stagger when I walk. You stay in the steam room long enough, you'll see God.

And after that, I'm relaxed for days. I go maybe once, twice a week. And no, I never take anyone there. The steam bath is someplace I can be, someplace I can just be.

The thing with women is that, sooner or later, they want to start buying slipcovers for the furniture. Let them in the door and the next thing you know you're being told to keep your shoes off of the couch. Your couch. And then you're done for, my friend, and then you're done for. Two things I never do: let a woman into my apartment, or let her know my real last name. That sounds harsh, okay. But that's the way it is. We can go out, we can party, we can fuck, but it never happens at my place. Sooner or later, they all start asking questions, of course, and it's time to say "so long." Which is a hell of a lot easier if they don't know your name or where you live, am I right? And, I'm getting to the point where I need them less and less. When I was younger, I'd wake up and think, "If I don't get laid today, I'm going to die." Now it's today, tomorrow, whenever. It's not the end of the world. You adjust. More than adjust, your priorities shift. Your needs change.

After I'd gone to the steam bath a few times, I saw that one guy was there more often than not. An older guy, maybe fifty or sixty, and built like a bear. A big hairy chest and a huge, hard stomach. Not fat, but big. Looking like you could swing a base-ball bat at him and it would bounce off. A big square head, and thick, furry eyebrows. I started thinking of him as "The Russian" because he looked like that Russian leader, the one before Gorbachev. Brezhnev. Yeah, there were a couple of others in between there, but no one else can remember them, so why should I? He looked like Brezhnev. And Jesus did he like it hot. It must be the Slavic blood, or something. The first time I walked in on him I didn't think I'd make it to the bench. The air was so charged with steam that I had to hold my hands over my mouth just to breathe. He sat there, holding onto the valve and stuking the steam, soaking it all up. I lasted about two minutes and then I had to leave. The Russian. Jesus.

There's one thing I'd better get out front, right now, and then leave it alone. I don't want to have to keep coming back to it, going into all the details that everyone gets wrong from all the hysterical movies they've seen and novels they've read. I'm under control, I'm not turning into a werewolf or anything, I'm not out killing grandmothers for their television sets. I manage just fine, thank you very much. So that's all I have to say. I'm not going into all the needle and spoon bullshit. For the record: no one knows about it, I'm very careful and completely under control. I don't have lines of tracks up and down my arms, that's all movie hype. Some people smoke cigarettes, some people have a gambling jones, the horses or the stock market, what does it matter? Me, I have this. So that's that.

Except to explain that that's another reason why I don't let women come over. Or anybody. You can't be too careful.

You would never know. You'll have to believe me on this, but it's true. In the steam-bath, naked, I can sit there and no one would ever know. I've got nothing to hide.

When I bought the gun, at first I didn't want any bullets. "So why not use a banana, no bullets?" I was asked. I thought about it and finally, yeah, I took the things. So it's loaded, yes, but I would never fire it. Never. That's one of those things you have to think about, ahead of time. Philosophy, if you like. You make the hard decisions with a cool head so that when the time comes . . .

You would be shocked how easy it is, and how cheap, to purchase a gun in this city. Better I should have it than some crazy kid. I wonder, sometimes, where it's all going. You have to wonder.

The Russian and I would nod when we saw one another. Usually he was there first, lost in the cloud of steam, his right hand pulling down on the steam valve. Only every now and again would I arrive before him, and then I'd be the one who sat in the corner, controlling the temperature. By this time I could bear it, at least survive. So I'd goose the heat, pulling down on the handle. The control was a rod sticking out of a hole in the wooden planks, and a chain attached it to a metal triangle that you pulled on. You'd think that the metal would be too hot to touch, but it actually felt cool. Funny. And you'd also think, from having watched the Russian pull down with one relaxed arm the size of my thigh, that it was easy. He'd pull that triangle all the way down and then sit there, roasting in the wet heat. With both hands I couldn't pull the thing down that far. Even so, I managed to get the place hot enough. Hot enough so that when the Russian came in he'd nod at me, and me at him, and then we'd sit, the only sound the hissing of the steam and the dripping of our sweat.

I don't go in for disguises – sunglasses, false beards, that sort of thing. Why not just wear a sign: hey, look at me, I'm a Bank Robber. My face is different. It's hard to explain, but when you think of yourself differently, your face changes. So that's what I do. When I walk into a bank, I'm a different person. You'd never recognize me.

The Russian started bringing in this little bottle. Eucalyptus oil. The first time he held it up and showed it to me. There were three or four others in the steam, but they were just transients, you know? The Russian and I were the two regulars, so he asked me. Held up the little bottle, cocked his thick Brezhnev eyebrows, and asked, "Okay?" He didn't sound like a Russian, of course. He sounded just like a regular guy.

I said sure, yeah, and he sprinkled a few drops out. The steam in my lungs turned into medicine, hot medicine. When you were sick, as a kid, did your mom have one of those vaporizer things? Vick's Vapor Rub. Maybe Vaporub, one word. When you were sick she'd spoon that stuff into a little steam machine, and the soothing steam would fix you right up, make you feel like you were living inside of something healthy. The eucalyptus smelled like that. I know what it is because I asked, and he passed the little bottle to me. "Good," I said, and he nodded. From then on, when I got there he'd pull out the little bottle, scatter a few drops. We'd nod at one another, smile. And then he'd pull down on that chain, fill the room with scalding menthol steam.

Last year in Vancouver there were one hundred and seventy-three bank robberies. I did seventeen of them. The trick is not to be greedy. You have a monthly budget, you manage your expenses, you plan. It's like any job: you know pretty well what your income is going to be, and you attempt to live within your means. And you do not get rich. My average take, averaged over the last five years, is $4,200 per job. That's tax free, of course, but you still see that it's not like on TV. I get by, and I keep my expenses steady, controlled. Of course I have a certain expense that I've already told you about, but I keep that steady, too. Pretty steady. I'll admit it can creep up on a person but it's nothing like you hear. People tell you stories: $500 per day, a week without sleep, $10,000 in one jag. Sure, it can be done, but it doesn't have to be that way. With a little discretion, and a little self-control, you'll have no problems.

What I like to do is go for a drink in a very fancy lounge. After, I mean. I walk away, turn a few corners, throw away the raincoat, recomb my hair, and then go to the Four Seasons piano lounge for a six-dollar beer. Sit and listen to an elegant black gentleman play subdued jazz on the piano. I like that. I sit there, my attaché case beside my stool, just another businessman enjoying some afternoon jazz. The last time, leaning against the teak bar, watching the thick black fingers ripple up and down the keys, the fellow next to me kept twiddling a cigarette back and forth between his fingers. He must have known that he was annoying the hell out of me, because he grimaced and said, "I'm trying to quit."

"Oh," I said. "It must be tough."

"Awful," he said. "You have no idea." He wanted to talk

more, but I turned away. After a little more jazz and one more beer I took a cab home. I got out of the cab a block away from my apartment and walked. It's one of my private little jokes that I live downtown, in the business section. Near all the banks. What the hell; you might say I was taking a chance, and you might be right, but I'd say I was having a bit of fun. And danger is always a part of fun, isn't it?

Spread out on the floor it didn't look like all that much, not measured in days and weeks. $6,500. That was three weeks ago and it's just about time again. It's just about time for me to go to work again.

I think both the Russian and I decided to wait the other out. It was the first time we arrived at the same time – I passed him in the changing room – and so we would be in the steam the same length of time. I think we both thought to ourselves, like kids do, "Let's see how far this other guy will go. Let's see." By the time he entered I'd managed to pull the lever all the way down. I made a discovery, then. You could wedge the metal triangle into the wooden slats so that it stayed there, all by itself, and the steam kept on and on. We sat, heads down, panting in the wet heat. Every now and then one of us would sit up, wipe sheets of sweat off his chest, his face, arms. We sat and the steam hissed, filling the room with a deep scorching fog.

We quit at the same time. We both stood up, shaking our heads, throwing in the towel. After my shower, after I'd changed and was leaving, he walked beside me and slapped me on the back. I laughed and shook my head. He shook his, both of us laughing at the two dumb pricks in the steam room. "See you," he said. "Take care."

"Stay cool," I said, and waved. I walked away and, waiting for the light to turn, saw him again a block away, tapping his attaché case against his leg, waiting for his light. He caught my eye, and we both shook our heads again, laughing.

I lied about the tracks. You always get tracks. But if you're careful, and smart, you get them in places that aren't obvious. So they're there, but even looking at them you wouldn't know what they are. I've probably lied about other things, as well. I'm in control of my life; I can do anything I want with it as long as I don't change it.

I waited patiently in line. I like Fridays. They're busy, everyone is bored and tired. And there's lots of money. So I stood, just another customer, moving my way forward place by place. That was always my favourite time, the waiting in line. You'd think it would be the moment with the most tension, the most fear. But in an odd way it was peaceful. As if I were in the right place, at the right time, and only I knew it. Everyone around me muttered and tapped their toes, impatient, but I was serene. Like a bridegroom in the hallway.

When I got to the teller I smiled and told her what I wanted. Never use a note, and never touch anything. I had to tell her again, I often do. People are never ready to hear that sort of thing, and their brains tell them: no, you misheard, listen again. So I told her again and she got that frozen, cat-in-the-headlights look they get, and then she slowly started taking money out of the drawer. They're well trained that way. And she was placing the bundles of bills into my attaché case, very carefully, very slowly, at great pains not to look at me, when I knew. Of course they have hidden alarms, but usually they're told not to touch them until we leave. But I knew. And I could hear the sounds in the bank change, so I knew something else, too. If I turned and looked I would see the police cars approaching. So I knew that, too.

I took out my gun, and the metal was cold in my hand, and heavy. I thought of the metal triangle, the one in the steam room. I had time to imagine it completely. "I'm going to leave, now," I told the girl, and she said, "Thank you." She thanked me.

I turned, with the gun in front of me. I pulled back the hammer so that it was ready. I walked slowly, calmly. I was wrong about the police cars. I didn't see or hear anything. If I could get out the door and around the corner, maybe I could get away, I would be safe. I reached to push the door with my attaché case. I kept the gun pointed, ready to do whatever I had to do. And as

I walked through the door I thought of the Russian. I thought of the Russian, hunched over on his wooden bench, looking up at me through his thick eyebrows, wondering if I could take any more steam.

LINDA HOLEMAN

Turning the Worm

Through the window over the kitchen table, Marianne can see the top of Shawna's head. The straight line of her scalp is gleaming white, and the shiny black hair hangs on either side of it like a thick still curtain.

Marianne stops on the top step of the back porch, wanting Shawna to lift her head, wanting to see the curtains part, see the lit stage of her daughter's face.

But even when she puts her key in the lock, turns it with a noisy scrape, Shawna's head stays bent over her book. It's not until Marianne pushes the door closed with a swoosh of air and a dull slam that Shawna lifts her head. Her eyes, wide, startled, stare at Marianne. Then her eyelids drop the tiniest fraction, and she studies her mother's face.

"How come *you're* home so early?" she asks, raising her hands to her ears. Marianne sees that she has her headphones on, but with the headpiece around the back of her head, instead of over the top.

"It's not early. Almost six. Didn't you read my note? I said I'd be back for supper." She glances at the table. "Homework on a Saturday?"

Shawna throws the earphones on the table beside her biology textbook, fiddles with the dials on her Walkman. "Early for *you*." Shawna's latest habit is to emphasize key words. "And it's not *homework*. I have a test on Monday, *remember*?"

"Right. I brought you something from Wendy's," Marianne

says, setting a white paper bag on the counter. "Tex-Mex chicken burger."

Shawna sighs. "I *told* you, Mother, I'm not *eating* that crap any more. You know what's *in* there."

"Oh, yeah. I forgot." Marianne opens the fridge. "There's not much here. I'll shop after work on Monday. What do you want for supper?" She doesn't look at Shawna as she takes a bottle of cranberry juice out of the fridge.

"I'm not hungry." A vertical furrow appears between Shawna's clear grey eyes as she watches her mother carry the Wendy's bag and the juice to the table and sit down across from her.

"I was *looking* for that sweatshirt."

Marianne opens the bag, pulls out a wrapped burger. "Sorry. You were asleep when I left." She pushes up the sleeves of the black Club Monaco sweatshirt and looks out the window over the table, shaking her head. "I should get started on the garden. It's almost too late to plant."

"I wasn't *asleep*," Shawna says. "I *heard* you."

"Well, you were lying on your bed with your eyes closed."

"I was listening to *Kurt*." Shawna raises her delicate chin towards the Walkman in front of her.

"I wish you wouldn't," Marianne says. "Listen to that stuff."

A small smile pulls up the corner of Shawna's mouth. "I'm not *that* stupid, Mother," she says to the Walkman. "Even if *all* of Nirvana committed suicide, I wouldn't." Then she looks at Marianne, and her pupils shrink into sharp points. Marianne starts fiddling with the empty paper bag, folding it carefully, into smaller and smaller squares. Then she puts her hands in her lap, pulling at the sweatshirt sleeves, pulling them down so the cuffs cover even the backs of her hands.

"What were you *doing*, all afternoon at Lloyd's? And was *he* there? *Dunc?*"

Marianne unwraps the burger, looks at it, then wraps it up again. She unscrews the lid of the juice, takes a drink. "Yeah, he was there. And we were just sitting around, watching TV. Some Grand Prix thing. Lloyd's into car racing." She takes another drink, nudges the burger with her knuckle. "I'm not really hungry either. We ordered pizza around two. I had pizza. And a Pepsi."

Shawna stands up and heads to the stairs leading off the kitchen.

"I did, Shawna. I told you it was for sure this time." Her voice rises half an octave. "I gave you my word."

The girl starts up the steps. Marianne tilts her head towards Shawna's thin straight back. "What, Shawna? What did you say?"

"*Nothing*," Shawna yells, the word bouncing and pinging against the wood panelling in the dark stairway.

"I heard you say something," Marianne calls, but only the dying echo of "nothing" answers her.

Marianne is asleep when the phone rings. She opens her eyes and blinks into the darkness, then turns on the lamp on the bedside table as she picks up the phone.

"'Lo," she says, clearing her throat, glancing at the clock. "Hello?"

"Mare? Hey Mare, honey, where'd you go? Where're you at?"

Marianne struggles to a sitting position, picking up her Rothmans from beside the phone. "I'm in bed, Dunc. It's after two." She taps the pack so the cigarettes and Safeway matches slide forward. Listening to the heavy ragged breathing on the phone, she clamps the receiver between her ear and shoulder and lights a cigarette.

"So, Dunc?" she says, blowing out a long, thin ribbon of smoke. She watches it wreathe around the lampshade and disappear into the shadows beyond the bed. As she drops the cigarette package back onto the table, she sees a miniature paper tent, a folded piece of lined white paper beside the lamp. She wonders how she missed it when she got into bed. She unfolds it and looks at what's written on the torn scribbler page, then lays it on her stomach.

"I woke up, and I didn't know where you were, Mare. I was all alone." The thick voice threatens to choke itself.

Marianne puts the cigarette between her lips, sits up straighter. She reaches out one finger and touches the paper.

"I just went home, Dunc. Remember? That's all. I just went home. I had to check on Shawna." The cigarette rises and falls in the clipped waves of her words.

"Can I come over?"

"Go back to bed, Dunc. Sleep it off." She waits. She can hear the blood pounding in her ear, pressed against the phone. "And Dunc?" She inhales, holds it while she counts to three, exhales. "Never mind."

"But I need you now, babe."

Marianne takes a coffee mug from beside the phone. She looks into it, then throws her cigarette into the scummy beige liquid. "No you don't. Now quit crying, and go to sleep." She slumps back against the pillow. "Everything'll be okay." Her voice is softer, slower, now. "It'll all be okay." It's the voice she used on Shawna, years ago. When Shawna still believed her when she said everything would be all right.

"It's okay," she murmurs, one last time, then gently places the receiver back on the hook, reaches down beside the bed and unplugs the phone. She looks at the paper again, smoothing out the one crease line, then props it against the lamp, and lies down on her side, her eyes fixed on the brief message.

On the way downstairs the next morning, Marianne glances into Shawna's room. She can just see the top of Shawna's head, in the mess of clothes and magazines and quilts.

Standing in the kitchen, Marianne drinks a glass of orange juice, but the inside of her mouth still feels dry, as if she's been running for a long time. She passes her tongue over her lips and goes out to the back yard, picking up the garden fork that's been leaning against the side of the house since the beginning of May.

At the edge of the rectangular weedy patch, Marianne puts the ball of her foot on the top of the fork, and pushes.

With a satisfying slide, the thick tines break through the hard topsoil. She turns the fork over, and breaks at the damp clumps of black dirt. She digs and turns again, and again, surprised at the richness of the soil under the surface. She feels a tight, almost pleasant pulling across her back.

When she turns over the fourth clump, she sees an earthworm burrowing frantically through the mud caught on the fork. She kneels and pulls off the fat, grey-pink worm, encased in wet dirt. She puts it into the cup of her hand, watching it work its way around the rough edges of her palm. She thinks about the day before, at Lloyd's, and about Dunc's voice, already loud and hoarse by the middle of the afternoon.

"Watch her. Hey, watch her, Lloyd. She'll eat the worm."

"Quit shittin' me, man."

"C'mon, Mare, eat the worm. Lloyd doesn't believe me."

Marianne had set her can of Diet Pepsi on the floor beside the couch and looked at the bottle of Mescal in the middle of the coffee table. The thick ribbed slug in the bottom of the bottle was magnified by the golden liquid.

"No."

"Do it, Mare." Dunc walked over to Marianne, sat down on the couch beside her. "Eat it, baby. Show Lloyd."

Marianne kept staring at the worm. "Cut it out, Dunc. I said no." She picked up the can of Pepsi, took a sip. "I only did it once, anyway."

Dunc hooted. "Who're you kidding? You did it more than once." He held up his hand, fingers outstretched. "That New Year's Eve party out at the cabin." He folded down his thumb. "When we were out in the boat, fishing with Rick." His index finger went down. "The time in Bemidji and, oh yeah," his third and fourth fingers bent over at the same time, "at your friend's place, what's-her-name, Mildred or whatever, from Safeway." He waved his little finger triumphantly.

"Millicent," she said.

"What?"

"Millicent. Her name was Millicent."

The little finger kept waving in front of her face. Dunc was grinning now. He picked up the bottle and rocked it from side to side. The worm floated upwards half an inch, then settled slowly and heavily to the bottom. "It's cawwwling you, Mare," Dunc said in a sing-song voice.

Marianne got to her feet. "It's calling *you*, Dunc." She looked down at him, at the thinning blond hair on the top of his head. "Eat the bloody worm yourself," she said, picking up Shawna's sweatshirt and pulling it over her head. "I'd rather have a Wendy's Classic."

Marianne looks at the squirming earthworm in her palm, then brings her hand to her face, and sniffs at the strong, cool odour of freshly dug soil.

The only worm she's smelled before was from the bottom of the bottle. Thinking about that other worm, her mouth is filled with a salty iron taste, but it's all confused with other tastes, tears and blood, and semen, on the back of her tongue, down her throat. Without warning, she turns her head and spits onto the ground beside her, and wipes her mouth with her bare arm. As she leans back on her heels, she hears a small rustle from the pocket of her cut-offs. She thinks about the lined paper there, of the two capital A's and seven-digit number, all in Shawna's clear round style. She remembers helping Shawna learn to print letters and numbers, her own big hand, steady back then, over Shawna's little-girl, almost boneless fingers.

Marianne picks up the worm and turns it over. It finally lies still, and she breathes in the clean dark smell again, inhaling deeply, as if her hand contains pure oxygen, as if it can take away the taste in her mouth.

Then she gently tips her palm, down, towards the garden. She sits on her knees, one hand fingering the paper in her pocket, and watches until the last tip of the pointed tail, like a satiny pink tongue, disappears, slipping beneath the surface smooth and easy as a cool sip of water on a hot day.

GREGOR ROBINSON

Monster Gaps

In the eyes of his parents Dearborn lived in a foreign country and it made him feel like an alien. How on earth would he tell them about Helen? He thought of himself as dutiful – he phoned every Sunday and between his mother and himself there were even occasional letters – but there was always reproach. Why had he left his home town? Dearborn said this was life in the twentieth century. People left towns and the countryside and moved to cities. People were in motion, not only in Ontario – he had only moved 170 miles, after all; they ought to put the matter in perspective – but across the globe. There was greed, fear, hatred, starvation. Immense economic and demographic forces were at work. Dearborn knew these things. He did specialized market research to earn his living.

That was another thing. "What is it you do, dear?" his mother would say. "People ask – your Aunt Adelle, friends – and I'm never able to explain. Not advertising, I know that. But something. What exactly? What do you *do?*"

His father had been a bank manager as had his father before him.

They were arriving that afternoon, staying three or four days. Dearborn had the details before him – his mother's clear handwriting on blue letterhead with a line drawing of the house where both he and his father had been raised. His grandmother had moved next door; his mother visited her every day until she died. His parents' lives made Dearborn feel insubstantial, like

149

the floating cotton from the big trees that grew by the stream at the end of the lawn.

They were coming to visit the children, his mother wrote. They thought it would be a help. They didn't know that the difficulty, as his mother always called it, was long over, had all been settled, really, the first year of the marriage.

And his father would visit doctors. He was being watched. For diabetes. For the arthritis that interfered with his walks. He drank too much. ("Eight ounces a day, I said to the doctor!" he'd told Dearborn the last time he was in the city, his eyes bright.) His heart. And the thing they avoided; his spells, his mother called it.

"Stupid!" Roxanne shouted. Dearborn looked up from his mother's letter, working the gap in his teeth with his tongue. "Careless girl!" Roxanne shouted. It was an expression of Anne's. (Dearborn used to admonish Anne: "Don't speak to the children like that. They'll pick it up.")

"Girls," he yelled. "Stop yelling."

("The reason they're always yelling," Anne would tell him, "is because *you're* always yelling. You should listen to yourself sometime.")

"We're not fighting," Roxanne yelled back from the living room. She was the older one, almost six. Jasmine was three and a half, liked to be called Dopey, like Snow White's dwarf. Jasmine and Roxanne.

"What kind of a name is Jasmine," Dearborn's mother had asked. "Are there Arabs somewhere back in our family? Am I missing something?"

Roxanne and Jasmine. Anne's choice. Dearborn would have named them Mary and Susan. One of the decisions over which he had not exercised his veto. The latest thing was that Anne wanted one of the girls. She said what difference did it make splitting them apart, since they were adopted anyway. He said this was creepy, and it was crazy; they were supposed to be a family.

"But we aren't a family any more," said Anne. "You and that teenager."

"She's not a teenager," he'd told her. "And you started it."

Almost true, Dearborn reflected. We order events according to our own mythologies.

Roxanne, walking around, now with one of the fat lamps in her arms: "It's all right, Sarah," she said to the lamp, "I'm here. Daddy's here."

"What are you playing?" Dearborn asked her.

"Big sister. This is the baby. Her name's Sarah."

"I told you, don't play with the lamps. Use a doll, the cat, something. You drop this lamp, you'll cut yourself."

"Is it made of china?"

"It's made of china. You know that," said Dearborn.

"It's precious, right?"

"Precious. Very precious, but not as precious as you." It was a discussion they'd had before. "Plus you could electrocute yourself pulling the plug."

Dearborn took the lamp and put it back on the table. He handed her one of the dolls from the armchair. But she'd already picked up the bookends, budgies in white marble. "It's all right, Sarah, don't cry," she said to one of the bookends. "Do you want to go to sleep? It's all right, you go to sleep. I'll be right here in the next room. I'll wear my big shoes, so you'll be able to hear me walking."

There was a note from the senior kindergarten teacher attached to the refrigerator door with a Pizza Hut magnet: Would the Dearborns please make a *special* effort to come on Monday? They wanted to talk about Roxanne.

Roxanne came into the kitchen. "Daddy, are you going to marry Helen?"

Dearborn shrugged; he couldn't talk, he was eating a muffin.

"Moon and June and kissing," said Roxanne. "Yuck," she turned and left, back to the living room, where Jasmine was monkeying with the cassette machine.

"Daddy, show us your monster laugh." Jasmine had sneaked up behind, through the dining room door.

During an argument on their first anniversary, Anne had reached across the glass table – they had crammed her patio furniture onto the tiny balcony of their twenty-first-floor apartment – and slapped Dearborn so hard she loosened an old tooth.

Now he had a crown, cloned on some fragment of the actual tooth. It kept falling out. He couldn't afford to go to the dentist every time, so he endured the gap. Did the monster laugh. For special occasions – nights out, meeting with clients – he shoved the tooth in with some chewing gum. It was usually good for two, perhaps three hours.

Roxanne came in with a tangerine. She wanted Dearborn to do Marlon Brando from *The Godfather*, another of his specialties.

"Not today, girls. The monster has a headache."

"You and Helen had too much wine, right daddy?"

Dearborn led them into the living room and put on a Three Stooges video.

"How could you have bought that for them," Anne had asked. "You think it's funny, hitting people over the head, sticking things up nostrils? You want them to grow up like that?"

Dearborn did think it was funny. And he hadn't grown up like that. What about your mother? She thinks farts are funny. Dearborn was at the stage where he was still framing responses, composing ripostes to old wounds.

Upstairs, Helen was sitting on the floor in the corner of the bedroom, playing with the cat. She was just out of the bathroom. She was wearing bikini underpants, no top.

"I love you," Dearborn told her. He bent down and kissed her left nipple. She smelled of his shower soap. "But you have to move your things out of the house."

She shrugged. "You're forty-four, right? Maybe it's time to tell them. Your parents. You know, like, you have a penis? You like girls?"

"You're only twenty-four. My mother is seventy-two."

"Great. Now we know everybody's age."

"They haven't taken it in that Anne is out of the picture. They think we might get back together."

"Doesn't matter to me. Really. I just think you should level with them. I don't believe in shame."

"It's not a question of shame," said Dearborn. "I just don't want them to know I'm involved so soon after my wife's departure with a woman twenty years younger."

"Like it might give them the wrong idea? I think they're old enough, you know?"

"How about your mother," Dearborn asked. "What does she think about us?"

"She likes you. She does. Anne first left, she wanted to ask you over for dinner? She wanted to go out with you herself. I think so. I really do. Get you in the sack."

"What about the age difference?"

"She's only two years older than you."

It wasn't just his imagination: he and Helen always seemed to be talking about people's ages. "I meant the difference between you and me," he said.

Helen's mother was on her own; her husband had just come out. "We used to wonder, like, why he never came home?" Helen had told Dearborn and Anne when she'd first found out. "Those walks in the park?"

"Another homo," Anne had said, glaring at Dearborn. She was at the stage where she still blamed everything on man, the species. She saw herself as enmeshed in a world of vile men.

Dearborn took Helen by the hand and pulled her up, towards the bed.

"I got class today," Helen said.

She taught gym, Saturday mornings. Dearborn told her he would give her a lift. Anne had left him the car. He'd won that argument: he needed the car for his work. In the end, when Anne moved out, Dearborn had quit his job and gone freelance. He now hated being out of the house, hated being away from the children, a complete reversal of poles. He stayed at home with the kids and his modem, Helen and teenagers from the neighbourhood helping out with the sitting. But he still had the car.

Before she got out, Helen said, "Warren called again."

Her ex-boyfriend. Warren Blue – he had invented his own name – played bass in a bar band. Otherwise, he did nothing. Dearborn would sometimes notice him loitering on the sidewalk in front of the house. Warren's career allowed plenty of time for watching and besetting. It was hard for Dearborn to understand how Helen had ever become involved with such a

person. She said it had started when she was in her freshman
year, when she hadn't had the confidence to say no. Warren Blue
was six foot three. No doubt he was tireless in bed, thought
Dearborn.

"Won't take no for an answer," he said.

"Won't take an answer, period," said Helen. "Bass players are
strange."

Dearborn took this as some kind of message, a vague threat.

"I'll tell my parents about us soon," he said. "Perhaps, before
they go home."

"See you tonight."

~

"Where are we going?" Dearborn's father asked. He gazed
around the hall. He had just left the TV room. He wore an old
tweed jacket with saggy pockets. His glasses were crooked.

"Maple Leaf Gardens," said Dearborn.

"Don't see why," said his father. "Don't see why we have to
go out."

"Jack, try to fit in," said Dearborn's mother. She held his coat
over her arm, waiting.

"You used to like hockey," Dearborn said.

"He still likes hockey," said his mother. "He watches on
television all the time."

"'Matlock' was just starting," said his father, somehow
vaguely affronted. He shuffled along to the bathroom. From the
hallway, Dearborn and his mother heard the click of the lock.
They heard him urinate. They heard a gurgling sound. Dearborn's father kept a bottle in his shaving kit.

"One good thing," said Dearborn's mother, "he's drinking
less. He forgets where he puts it. He forgets that he likes it."

His father opened the bathroom door. He positively beamed.
"Hockey!" he said. "They've finally started to win."

Downstairs, Helen was waiting in pressed faded jeans and a
black ribbed turtleneck. Her hair was glossy. She would be sitting the children.

"I'm glad to meet you at last. I've heard so much about you,"
Helen said when Dearborn introduced her to his parents.

"You have?" said his mother, glancing at Dearborn. She had eyes like a hawk.

After the game, Dearborn took them out for a coffee. The restaurant was brightly lit with huge orange globes over brown-and-orange decor. The place was crowded and the manager sat them at a big table with a father and two young boys. The boys looked remarkably like the father, Dearborn noticed. As he aged, he took note of family resemblance more and more. He was becoming something of an expert on nature versus nurture, the various theories. What effect would divorce have on his children, he wondered.

The two boys had souvenir programs from the game spread on the table.

"Good game," said Dearborn's father, smiling at them.

The boys nodded.

"I used to play for the Leafs," said Dearborn's father.

Was this true, Dearborn wondered. His father had played for McGill, before the war, and Dearborn remembered something about his father having been asked to try out for the pros. But nothing more, surely.

"Yeah?" said the older boy. He would have been about nine.

"Wicked," said the younger, about six.

"Yup," said Dearborn's father. "Played with Eddie Shore and Turk Broda. Teeder Kennedy."

The boys' father looked at Dearborn's father in studied silence. The boys were silent too. Perhaps the way Dearborn and his mother were watching, waiting to see what would happen next, gave them a signal.

"Johnny Bower. Gordie Howe. All the greats," said Dearborn's father.

"Johnny Bower?" said the older boy, puzzled.

"Really," said the man. He definitely knew now that the chronology was impossible. He was young, maybe twenty-eight. Dearborn noticed that he had the same kind of intonation, used the same expressions as Helen.

"When did Gordie Howe play for the Leafs?" the older boy asked his father. "Gordie Howe never played for the Leafs."

"Eat your cake," the father answered.

"Is that guy weird, or what?" asked the six-year-old, half-whispering.

Dearborn's father looked down at his coffee. He took off his glasses; his eyes were red-rimmed. Dearborn thought his father might weep, and he put his hand on his arm.

"I think I'll go downstairs and have a pee," said his father, with immense dignity. Dearborn and his mother watched him shamble towards the kitchen. He looked up at the clock on the wall, stopped, then kept on towards the kitchen door. The boys beside them watched too, clearly fascinated by a man who became lost in a restaurant.

"I think you'd better go with him," said Dearborn's mother.

On the way home, she sat in the front seat, talking about the town where he had grown up, people he had known when he was a child. "You heard about Henry Rollins," she said, looking at him sideways. "He's up at Penetang, locked up. He was in a variety store. He fell asleep standing up at the magazine rack. That's what he does, you know, falls asleep standing up. Happens all the time. When the owner woke him up, Henry stabbed him. So the police came and they took him up to Penetang." Henry Rollins was Dearborn's age. He was adopted.

After a few moment's silence, Dearborn's mother said, "It's not Helen, is it?"

"It's not Helen what? She babysits."

"Old to be a babysitter," said his mother.

"Not that old."

"Not that old – you're right about that. She can't be more than twenty-five."

In the rearview mirror Dearborn saw his father put his finger in his ear and shake it with a vigour that made him wonder his father didn't dislodge his own yellow teeth. His mother noticed too; she turned and gave Dearborn a look. The finger-in-ear business – it was a sign, a warning flag in their family. Dearborn's father did not like discussions about personal matters. He preferred undercurrents.

"Good God," he said, looking out the window. "Do you see?"

"What?" said Dearborn's mother.

"The people. Where are we? Africa? Pakistan? Where do they come from? Why do we let them in? Used to be a perfectly good country."

"You and Anne, you should never have moved down here," said Dearborn's mother, ignoring this diversion.

"Mother, grow up."

"I'm seventy-two. How much more grown up do you want me?" She sighed heavily. "All right, I accept this divorce business, although I never thought we'd have it in our family. Perhaps now you'll have children of your own." Her family had been in Ontario since the American Revolution.

Dearborn glanced up and caught his father looking at him in the mirror; there was a momentary bright look in his eyes; he was with them again, had broken through the haze of whisky, the floating cobwebs, the ganglions in his brain. He said, "He already has his own children. Bonny children they are, too."

They drove the rest of the way in silence. When Dearborn pulled into the driveway, his father said, "You have a garage?" He knew perfectly well they had a garage; Dearborn had parked the car there – it was halfway behind the house – when he'd brought them back from the bus station.

"I would like to see the garage," said his father.

"Don't tell him how to get into the garage," said Dearborn's mother under her breath.

"Door halfway down the basement stairs," said Dearborn. His father nodded, turned to shuffle up the front steps. He would be getting something from his shaving kit, a stash to hide in the garage for the duration of the visit. He kept bottles in the garage at home. Wherever he went he liked to establish a safe haven. Dearborn's mother glared at him, and Dearborn was suddenly enraged again. This was a recent phenomenon, the rage that seemed to come in waves. Dearborn said to his mother, "If he wants a drink he can have one."

The truth was his father didn't actually drink that much any more, certainly less than Dearborn. He simply liked the routines, the hiding bottles and so on, and Dearborn understood that.

On Monday evening Dearborn stood before the bathroom mirror, affixing his tooth in the gap with a big wad of gum in preparation for the visit to the school. He could hear the television from the den along the hall where his parents were watching the six o'clock news. Then he heard different noises. Someone entering the house. Could it be Helen, ignoring his warnings? The door from the porch closing quietly. The footsteps stopped. Intruders! Teenagers, no doubt. Dearborn's heart raced. He poked his head in the door of the den. His parents sat staring at the television; they had heard nothing. He told them he was going to check the casserole. He crept down the stairs.

It was only Warren Blue, six foot three and skinny as a rail, standing in the middle of the kitchen. He wore a greasy buckskin jacket that hung shapeless from his shoulders. "Where's Helen?" Warren stepped towards Dearborn, as though he were going to push by him and make his way upstairs to the bedrooms. He looked angry; his face was blotchy.

Dearborn said, "No need to get riled up."

"Fuck you," said Warren.

Upstairs, there was a stirring, Dearborn's father on one of his trips to the bathroom. Then his mother's shoes along the hall floor; the footsteps grew silent, muffled as she descended the carpeted stairs. Weren't they supposed to be hard of hearing?

"She's not here, Warren. I'm sorry. I think she said something about an aerobics class. If I see her, I'll tell her you're looking for her. Listen, I have guests. I think you'd better go."

Dearborn made a move towards the back door, to show him out. Warren grabbed Dearborn's arm, twisted him around and slapped him across the face, as though Dearborn were a cheeky school girl. Dearborn's hand shot out in a reflex movement, a light shove to Warren's chest. Warren responded with a real punch, a blow to Dearborn's mouth that nearly knocked him off his feet. He tasted salty blood and salty tears; the tears were not tears of emotion, nor tears of engagement; they welled up involuntarily with the pain. He felt the gap in his teeth with his tongue. His mouth was filling with blood.

Suddenly the room was filled with people. His parents hovering behind him – it appeared that they could move fast and

quietly when they wanted to – the children up from the basement, and Helen bobbing behind Warren in the back door.

Roxanne said, "Daddy, are you going to need a needle?"

Jasmine saw the blood and began to weep.

Dearborn said, "Mother, dad, this is Warren Blue, a neighbour
of ours. And Helen, you know Helen of course."

"The babysitter," said Dearborn's father. "Delighted to see
you again. Are we going out?"

"I've seen you walking up and down the sidewalk in front of
the house," Dearborn's mother said to Warren Blue.

Warren and Helen looked at each other. She put her arm on
his back, running her hand up underneath his buckskin jacket.
She seemed to whisper something, calm him down. Then he
turned, her fingers grazing along his back as they walked
through the door.

Dearborn knew then he would not have to face the problem
of how to tell his parents about Helen. She was going back to
Warren. It was simply a matter of when.

"That was something," his father said. "Never seen a fight
before."

"Very stupid," said his mother. "You're far too old for this
sort of thing."

It was true, he was too old. And his father was wrong: it
wasn't a fight. It was Dearborn standing there, and Warren hitting him in the mouth. It was as though it had happened to
another person.

His mother appeared with a wet washcloth. When Dearborn
examined himself in the mirror, he saw that blood was coming
from the gap where he had jammed the tooth in. Usually when
it came loose, he caught the tooth rolling around in his mouth,
an immense foreign object. This time it was gone. He phoned
the dentist, a neighbour, who told him to stuff a piece of cotton
batting into the gap. The flow of blood would likely stop in a few
minutes. Dearborn asked him about the tooth.

"This too will pass," said Dr. More.

"What?"

"You probably swallowed it. You could sift through, you
know, after you go to the toilet."

"Absolutely not. Out of the question," Dearborn told him.

"At least a thousand bucks to do a new one and put it in," said Dr. More.

Dearborn would live with the gap. He cleaned himself up. He left his parents in front of the television eating the casserole.

The school evening was set up so the children could greet parents at the door and show them around. There were big scrapbooks filled with drawings, scraggly numbers and alphabets. Then the pictures. The teacher would add the titles afterwards. ("What's this a picture of, sweetie?" "Daddy playing monster.")

Ms. Fish, the efficient one, was there by the desk to greet him. Tall, about thirty-eight, red hair done up with elaborate clips. The old friendly one, Mrs. Wesley, stood a few feet behind, clasping her hands. She reminded Dearborn of his grandmother. She hugged the children when they came in the morning.

Mrs. Fish took him aside. "Will your wife be joining us?"

"No," said Dearborn.

"Yes," said Anne. She came hurrying towards them, wispy blonde hair plastered across her forehead.

"What are you doing here?" said Dearborn.

"They called me about Roxanne."

"Why would they call you?"

"Roxanne talks to things," said Ms. Fish, quiet and solicitous.

The wave came: Dearborn was enraged. He listened to his wife and Mrs. Fish talking about Roxanne. He grabbed Ms. Fish by the wrist. He could feel the heat in his face. No doubt the vein in his forehead was sticking out.

Anne said, "Jack, take it easy. It's not serious, only mild troubles, they said."

"Mrs. Fish," said Dearborn, still holding her by the wrist.

"Ms.," said Ms. Fish.

"Mrs. Fish," said Dearborn. "I am aware that Roxanne talks to things. I live with her. She talks to lamps. She talks to bookends. She calls them Sarah. I am her father. I talk to things myself."

Other conversations in the room stopped.

"Mrs. Fish." Should he tell her everything, that the girl's

mother had left despite her presence here tonight, that Roxanne was adopted, that he'd swallowed his tooth, that his father became lost on the way to the washroom in restaurants? Should he tell her about the inevitability of Helen and Warren Blue? "Mrs. Fish." Dearborn was aware that he was speaking through clenched teeth. "Do not speak of psychologists and professionals in front of my child."

"Oh, God," said Anne.

Dearborn turned; he picked up the children at the Play-doh table and fled from the room. In the parking lot, they sat in the dark car, waiting for the defroster to clear the windows. He was exhausted. He was half asleep. His legs ached. His gap ached.

Roxanne said, "Daddy, what are you thinking?"

He didn't tell her. He was watching himself walking around the house, talking to the fat lamp, sifting through his own waste for some forty-year-old remnant.

On the radio, they were playing some kind of torch music.

Roxanne said, "Hey, hot lips." It was a mystery to Dearborn where these expressions came from. There was a new one every day.

"Poo-poo head," said Jasmine.

"Girls," said Dearborn, in warning.

Roxanne said, "Daddy, can I be the man of the house?"

"Who makes the hardest hugs?" said Jasmine, hugging him.

"Who makes the softest hugs?" said Roxanne, also hugging him. They sat tangled in the front seat of the car.

DAVID ELIAS

How I Crossed Over

Our village was so close to the border that a south-bound traveller had no sooner left the shade of the last cottonwood tree than he bumped right up against the United States of America. The road leading through the village ended abruptly, cut off by a grassy ridge that ran dead-straight for as far as you could see in either direction.

The only thing to do was turn around and go back. Unless, of course, crossing over was exactly the reason you'd come that way in the first place. Then you could just go right ahead and cross. There was no one – and nothing – to stop you.

The elders of the village had posted no guards. They figured that by the time you were old enough to think about leaving, you were old enough to know you didn't belong any place but the valley, especially any place on the other side of that ridge. You didn't dress right or talk right or even think right to fit in there. You picked it up from people like Bill's older brother, who just last summer struck out on his own, and was back inside of a month, silent and timid, and with never quite the same look in his eye.

The ridge itself was no obstacle at all. Five steps up, five across the top, and five more down the other side. That was all there was to it. Once across, you could make your way over the open fields and look for a road to follow.

But after you'd been down one or two, you realized that things were different here. This land wasn't cut up into neat squares, the way you were used to, with a cross-roads every mile to tell you how far you'd come, and show you the four points of the compass. Roads here ran in no particular direction, and for no set distance. The one you picked might go on for miles, or only as far as the next stand of trees.

But then, just when you were beginning to think about turning back, you found a highway and followed it until the lay of the land began to look familiar. There was a turn-off you remembered because of the sign: Preston Potato Growers, and when you finally saw the fields you'd worked in only a few weeks ago, you breathed easier and made your entrance as casual as it needed to be.

Stroll up the drive and into the big yard in behind the trees. Pet the dog when it comes down off the white porch, barking just enough to let folks know there's a visitor – a dog that remembers the scent of your hand from the sandwich you fed it that first day, too tired to eat it yourself, half asleep under that big tree – right there – at the edge of the field.

Past the window of the big house ready to smile if someone should come to the curtains. Along a row of bins and into a bunkhouse to find the mattresses rolled up and stacked by the door. Walk between the bare steel frames of the double bunks on either side, until you reach a door at the far end of the room – a door that isn't quite shut, but isn't quite open either – and instead of knocking, sense the emptiness on the other side, and push the door wide.

This wasn't the way you'd worked things out, lying awake those nights, figuring how Solly's face would be there to greet you – how the words would sound between his white teeth when he asked, "Now what in the world are you doin' back here, son. You must have left somethin' pretty important behind." And you wouldn't say anything because what you'd come back for would be in your eyes and he'd see it, and just smile, and open the door for you to come in.

But now the bare room holds only the naked frame of another bunk, a chair, and there on the painted table, the wooden spoon that shows a row of notches carved along the handle, the one farthest up fresher than the others. You pick it up and play your fingers slowly over the notches.

You lay the wooden spoon back on the table and go back out the way you came in. Up to the house with the big window to wait for a woman to come to the door and tell you that Solly only ever stayed until picking time was over, and wouldn't be back now until the spring, and maybe not even then, if he decided to go and live with his son like he'd said he might. And had you come all the way on foot, and could she bring you something cold to drink because it was a long way back and did your mother know what you were up to?

It was just a few weeks ago that the truck came rolling into the village, the way it did every fall, honking a few times as it coasted slowly along under the tall cottonwoods, crunching to a stop halfway up the street. Pretty soon people would come wandering over, a bag or two in hand, to talk to the driver a minute before they jumped up onto the back of the open truck box.

We'd all been expecting the truck to come any day. It was harvest time, and that meant the big American potato farmers would be up looking for pickers. All they had to do to get them was drive across the line and find the nearest village, which happened to be ours, and there was all the cheap labour they could get their hands on.

Potato picking across the line was one of the few freedoms the elders didn't mind granting us. It was all right with them, just that one time in the year, for us to venture out into the world, so long as we were going there to do backbreaking work for almost no pay.

It was my year to go, so I hopped on with the others. Bill would have gone, too, in a minute, but he wasn't old enough yet, so he'd have to wait until next year. I didn't mind it all that much him not coming. We did everything together, and it wasn't so bad to be striking out on my own for once.

When the truck started back out of the village, I shouted and waved to Bill where he sat on the bridge, his feet dangling over the side. He finally waved back just before we turned west, heading for the highway.

At the border, I heard the customs officer say, "I should be asking you for papers on every one of these boys, you know that, don't you, Harley?"

The driver passed him an envelope. He took it and said, "I just hope none of them is in any trouble up there." He was wearing a gun on his hip, so I figured he'd sure know trouble if he saw it. At least I hoped he would.

"Why, these boys wouldn't know trouble if it came up and bit 'em on the ass," said the driver. "Most of 'em probably never been out of the valley. And you know all they ever do there is sit and spit." The driver spat, just for effect, and they both laughed before the truck started up again.

I sat down after that, partly because we were soon going fast enough for the grasshoppers to sting my face, and partly because I was thinking about what the driver said.

It wasn't long before we turned off the highway, at least it didn't seem like it, sitting down low in the truck box like that, with only the sky to watch. Then it was just a few minutes down a gravel road and we were there.

We hopped off the back of the truck and they didn't give us more than a minute to look around before they got us to put our things in the bunkhouse and fed everyone and then we were out in the fields picking potatoes. A black farmhand kept us supplied with burlap sacks, and marked it down every time we filled one in a little book he pulled out of his overall pocket. When he came up next to me that first time, I stopped long enough to notice the black and white curls on the top of his head, and then the deep brown forehead underneath when he looked back up from his writing.

That evening, riding back in, sitting on my potato sacks, I heard him singing inside the cab of the truck. His voice, mixed in with the drone of the engine, made the words come out thick and deep:

Baahh-n-baahh
Wen thuh moanin cuhmmm
Wenn awll thuh saynnts-a-gawd
Gatheh et ho mmmm

Thehn wee tehll thu stow-ree
Juss haa wee ohvuhcuhmmm
Enn wee undehstan ip bedduh
Baahh-n-baahh, Lohd, baahh-n-baahh

Back in the bunkhouse – the evening meal over and sleep only minutes away – I counted up what I'd be paid for the day and thought about that singing, about how it sounded so sad and hopeful all at the same time. I was trying to remember how the melody went, humming quietly to myself, when Solly (I picked up his name when Mr. Preston called him over while we were unloading) came striding through on his way to his room at the far end of the bunkhouse. He walked in a way that was tired, but not worn, that made me think he could still get his hands on plenty of strength, if he had to. He smiled at me when he went by, eyes shiny, and closed the door quietly after him.

The next thing I knew he was tapping on the steel frame of my bunk with a wooden spoon, yelling, "WE got to get up now boys. Taters ain't cotton but WE got to pick 'em just the same. WE got to pick 'em and bag 'em and haul 'em in." It was almost like singing, the way he did that, but it was talking, and somehow I didn't mind so much getting up so early. Pretty soon everybody was dressed and ate some cakes and then it was onto the truck and out into the fields again.

It was like that every day for a week, except Sunday. We'd just as soon have worked that day, too, but if it ever got back to the village that they'd put us to work on The Sabbath, even if we were just a bunch of squirmy Mennonite boys, well then next year when the truck came through the village it would leave as empty as it came in. The same thing would happen when they drove on to the next village, and the one after that. That was the way they worked things in our valley.

So naturally we had to take the day off and everyone was headed for a swimming hole that some of the older boys knew about, and I'd have gone too, if it hadn't been for the music that filtered out of Solly's room at the end of the bunkhouse, just as I was about to follow the others out. It was the same kind of

thing that Solly'd been singing in the cab of the truck every
night, only now it was someone else singing, and I could hear a
piano with it. I told the others I'd be along in a minute, and for
them to go ahead without me.

The music came louder and fuller as the bunkhouse emptied,
until there was just the music, coming down out of the rafters,
like in church, except this wasn't like any church singing I'd ever
heard. I was used to elders up at the front, setting out the tune
for the congregation to follow – a tune that was never more than
a few notes away from the hymn before it, or the one after.

My grandfather liked to say how you could take comfort in
singing like that, but the problem was, there was just no give to
it. It just went on and on, verse after verse, until about the only
comfort you could take was to know that things were that much
closer to being done for another Sunday.

But this singing had a string woven through that pulled me
along, drew me closer, until – without meaning to – I was at the
door of Solly's room. When it opened, Solly asked over the
music, "How come you ain't swimming with the others?"

"The singing," I said. "I was listening to the singing."

He looked at me – different than before – and said, "Come on,
then."

I stepped inside and sat down on the end of the bunk bed,
watched him turn a black record over in his hands to read the
label before placing it carefully on the old turntable. "This is the
queen." He brought the needle down gently. "This is Mahalia.
Listen now." Through the scratching – singing over a hollow,
distant piano – came a voice solid oak:

Move on up a little higher, Lord
Meet with old man Daniel
Feast with the Rose of Sharon

And it'll be always "howdy howdy"
It'll be always "howdy howdy"
Say it'll be always "haaaaowdy howdy"
And never "good-bye."

That voice, and the notes it sang, and the words of that music, all went right through my ribs and into my chest – started a warming deep inside there, until I felt something coming up like crying or laughing or maybe shouting, and I wasn't sure which it was going to be except that it was coming. I knew right then that it was something I'd always yearned for, somehow – like a newborn baby taking its first mouthful of sweet warm mother's milk, and realizing that all along the way to being born, it had longed after the taste of that very thing.

Then it was over and there was nothing but the scratching and the sound of Solly's voice from his chair, looking over at me. "It moved you, son." His eyes were so bright. "I can see that. It moved you just the same."

We listened all through that afternoon. Solly called out everything before setting it on the turntable. There was the Angelic Gospel Singers, and the Golden Gate Jubilee Quartet, the Soul Stirrers, and the Dixie Hummingbirds. And when they sang, they asked you to do things, like sing along, or clap your hands, or be a witness.

So pretty soon, when Brother Joe May said he needed someone to help him call Mary, I followed Solly's lead, and called with him. And later, when the Swan Silvertones asked for a witness, we did that too, until the two of us were dancing through the door and out between the bunks, hands in the air and me so far outside myself I didn't care if I ever got back.

Then everyone was back from swimming and Solly hurried in and took the needle off. I stayed out with the others and told them I fell asleep, but the whole time I was taking a ribbing and hearing what a good time I missed, I was thinking about how I could get another chance to listen to that music.

The way I figured it, the best I could hope for would be next Sunday. I set it in my mind to wait that long and every day after that the work got a little easier, just thinking about Sunday, but then the picking was done and it was only Friday and before I even had a chance to figure something out they had us back up on the truck and heading over the border.

Riding out over the cab, singing quiet notes into the wind, I didn't care about any grasshoppers stinging my face. I wanted to get a better look at where I'd been. I already knew I was coming back, one way or the other.

Back in the village again, sitting through another Sunday in church, all I could do was remember. And when the hymns went on for too long, the way they always did, I'd be only a commandment away from jumping up off the hard wooden pew – up from behind the kerchiefs and collars – to yell, "Clap your hands, you sinners, and listen to this!"

It wasn't long before Bill got it out of me about Solly and the music and everything.

"That must have been some fancy singing, to make you talk about it like that."

"Not fancy, exactly."

"Well, what then?"

"I don't know."

"Well, what made it so special?"

"Nothing, I guess. I don't know. It's hard to explain."

Bill was quiet for awhile. Then he said, "I know what you have to do."

"What's that?"

"You have to sing me some."

I shook my head. "It just wouldn't be the same."

"The same as what?"

"The same as it was."

"Sing just a little bit of it. Just so I get the idea."

So later that afternoon, down along the creek bed, on what turned out to be the last warm day in October, I sang him some – sang it the best way I knew how – the way Solly would have sung it – right up out of my insides – and that way maybe I could at least get the spirit of the thing across.

It was hard to tell how Bill was taking it, the way he just stared, like he might pull some seeds out of his shirt and start cracking, or maybe walk away, just spitting and shaking his head. Sometimes things could just run off Bill like water off a grease patch.

But he didn't take out any seeds. He didn't turn and walk. He just stayed quiet another minute, and then he said, "Teach me."

So I taught him a part about where you ask for a witness, and he caught on right away. Then he was clapping and singing, and it wasn't like I was showing him any more, but like it moved him that way, and that's when I knew he'd got it, too.

We spent the better part of that last warm afternoon drinking that healing water ("all God's sons and daughters") and telling Mary she didn't have to weep ("'cause Pharaoh's army got drowned in the sea") and singing always "howdy howdy" and never "good-bye."

I didn't think it'd go any further than that, but then Sunday in Bible Study Class, when Miss Friesen, the shiny-faced teacher, asked the way she always did, "Now, boys and girls, what shall we sing to close today's lesson?" Bill put up his hand and said, "We know one but you never heard it." He gave me that look he always had when he was playing around. His eyes were saying there was a chance here, and didn't I want to take it? Didn't I want to go?

"Oh," said Miss Friesen. "Well, perhaps you could teach it to us."

"Sure," said Bill. "We'll sing it for you. Steve and me."

"Will we be able to join in?" Miss Friesen wanted to know.

"Oh, yes, ma'am," Bill said. "We want you to join in, right Steve?"

I nodded weakly.

"Very well, then." She straightened her skirt over her lap. "Now, boys and girls, pay close attention. William and Steven are going to teach us a new song."

So there we were, the two of us, up at the front of the room, looking over at each other and then down at the others and then over at the teacher, because neither of us had ever done anything in Sunday Bible Study Class but pull pigtails and make rude noises and here we were up at the front of the class and not only that but we were going to sing.

Bill looked at me, and I could see that he'd pretty much lost his nerve, like he'd just as soon sit back down and let the whole thing pass. I stared back at him for maybe a full minute, or what seemed like it.

"Milky White Way," I said, and started in.

I'm going to walk – *clap walk*
That Milky White Way – *clap* (Oh child)
Some of these days – *clap walk clap walk*

Bill pulled himself together and joined in.

Yes, Yes, I'm going to walk – *clap walk*
That Milky White Way – *clap walk*
Oh some of these days – *clap* – well, well (well well)

One of the girls, from her place on the floor, began to clap quietly along. Then another joined in, and after that a couple of the boys, and I figured if we just kept at it they'd be up and moving soon enough. It wasn't hard to see how Miss Friesen was taking it. Her shiny face lost all of its colour, and she clutched at the lace around the neck of her blouse, but by then the spirit was moving in me, and I let it take me, so it didn't matter about Miss Friesen or anybody else.

I didn't even realize she'd left the room until she stepped back in through the doorway, the preacher and several of the elders close behind. They stood there, silent and fierce, and that was all they had to do. It was enough to put an end to everything.

They sent everyone home, except for Bill and myself, and when the others were all gone they took us to a room at the very back of the church and left us there to listen at the door while they exchanged words in Low German, their voices slow and deliberate.

"What was that there what they singing did?"

"That acquaint I not, but it listens me altogether cracked."

"Well, you know, that hears me like nigger music."

"Nigger music? Mean you?"

"I believe, yes."

"But where have they that learned?"

"That holds now all sausage, but it must right away discontinue."

We got back to our chairs just before they came in to stand over us in a half-circle of frowns.

"Now, boys," the preacher began, "tell us where you learned such singing?"

"No place," I said quickly, and louder than I expected. I looked over at Bill, hard. Now it was my turn to tell him here was a chance, and didn't he want to go?

"That's right," said Bill. "No place at all."

"No place," the preacher echoed. "So you just made it up."

"We didn't exactly make it up," said Bill. "It just kind of came to us."

"Came to you, did it?"

"That's right."

"I will only say this once," said the preacher. "Unless you answer truthfully, it will only be worse for you."

"We didn't know it was wrong," said Bill. "We wouldn't have done it if we knew it was wrong." He was on a roll now, so I could just sit back and let him go. "We were only praising the Lord. Make a joyful noise unto the Lord. That's what it says in the Bible, doesn't it?"

The preacher got very red, then, and looked over at the others. "This is the work of the devil," he said, "when boys quote scripture to twist their way out of trouble." He turned to Miss Friesen and the others. "You're excused," he said. "I'll handle it from here."

As soon as I heard that, I knew we were in for a heavy strapping, so we didn't have to try and explain any more, or worry about letting on the way it really was. We could just give it up and let things take their course.

Bill was first and took to howling so that anyone in earshot would have thought he was being murdered, just like he always did in school. His way of thinking was that if you were going to get a strapping anyway, you might as well get some mileage out of it.

Then it was my turn. I wasn't sure how I'd take it, but after the first few lashes – watching the stiff black leather sting into my hand, turning it blue and puffy – I knew they could never beat it out of me. Not the best part of it. Not the part that made

me want to laugh and cry at the same time, like I was doing now.
That poor preacher had no way of knowing that with every blow
he delivered, he was only sealing it farther inside me.

I was strapped into a promise never to sing anything like that
again, anywhere, but I knew – even before my tears had dried –
that sometime soon, maybe on a Sunday, I'd wander out to the
edge of the village and over the ridge, and when I was sure it was
safe, I would fill my lungs and sing:

How I crossed over,
How I crossed over,
My soul'll look back and wonder
How I crossed over.

About the Authors

Rick Bowers teaches in the department of English at the University of Alberta. His fiction has appeared in *The Antigonish Review* and the *Pottersfield Portfolio*. A collection of his stories, *The Governor of Prince Edward Island*, was published by Pottersfield in 1986. More recently, his work has appeared in the NeWest collection, *Boundless Alberta* (1993). He is currently developing stories for a new collection.

David Elias was born and raised in a Mennonite farming community near the U.S. border in southern Manitoba. Orca Books has published a collection of his short stories under the title *Crossing the Line*. "How I Crossed Over" is the title story for a new manuscript of short fiction just completed. He lives with his wife, Jessie, and three children in Winnipeg, Manitoba.

Elyse Gasco has published work in *The Malahat Review*, *Canadian Fiction Magazine*, *Grain*, *Prism international*, and other magazines. She has recently completed a collection of short stories, and the story printed here is one in a series of linked pieces. She lives in Montreal.

Danuta Gleed was born in Kenya, in a British camp for displaced persons where she spent her early childhood. In 1958, she moved to England with her family. She now lives in Ottawa and has studied writing with Frances Itani, Audrey Thomas, Bryan Moon, and Rita Donovan. She has been published in many literary journals and has been a winner in several short-story competitions. Many of her stories draw on her Polish background. She hopes to have her first collection completed soon.

Elizabeth Hay's most recent book is *Captivity Tales: Canadians in New York*. Her story "Hand Games" was included in the previous edition of *The Journey Prize Anthology*, and was short-listed for the Journey Prize. That story and "The Friend" are part of a new collection of stories to be published by The Porcupine's Quill in the spring of 1997. She lives in Ottawa.

Linda Holeman's works include a collection of young-adult stories, *Saying Good-bye* (Lester Publishing, 1995), a children's novel, *Frankie on the Run* (Boardwalk Books, 1995), and an adult-fiction collection, *Flying to Yellow* (Turnstone Press, 1996). Linda won the 1995 Thistledown Press Young Adult Short Story competition, and *Saying Good-bye* was a finalist for the 1996 McNally Robinson Book for Young People Award. Forthcoming from Tundra Books is a YA novel. Linda is currently completing another adult-fiction collection. She lives in Winnipeg.

Elaine Littmann lives in Vancouver and works as a graphic designer. Her fiction has been published in several journals, and appears in the anthology of young women's writing *eye wuz here* (Douglas & McIntyre, 1996).

Murray Logan will be featured in Oberon Press's *Coming Attractions* anthology, to be published in the fall of 1996. His first book, a collection of short stories, will be published in the spring of 1997 by The Porcupine's Quill. He lives in Vancouver.

Rick Maddocks was born in South Wales and emigrated to Canada in 1981, where he grew up in the heart of Ontario's tobacco belt. His stories have appeared in *The Fiddlehead* and *Event*. He now lives in Vancouver, where he works as a fiction editor and performs with his band, No Soap Radio. He is currently assembling a collection of stories.

K.D. Miller lives in Toronto. She has published short fiction in *WRIT*, *Flare*, *The New Quarterly*, and *The Capilano Review*. She has twice before been included in *The Journey Prize Anthology*. Her first collection of short fiction, *A Litany in Time of*

Plague, was published by The Porcupine's Quill in 1994. She is currently working on a second collection of stories, of which "Egypt Land" is the title story.

Gregor Robinson is a graduate of the University of Toronto and the London School of Economics. His stories have appeared in *Descant*, *Grain*, *The New Quarterly*, *Queen's Quarterly*, *Ellery Queen's Mystery Magazine*, and elsewhere. *The Dream King*, a collection of his short fiction, will be published in 1997. He lives in Toronto.

Alma Subasic lives in Toronto with her partner, Allan Sanders, and is finishing an M.A. in English at York University. She plans to finish her novel, *Dust*, by December 1996 and submit it for publication. She and Allan are compiling a book on "candida albicans," a yeast overgrowth problem that affects millions of people in North America. She has begun work on a second novel which, she says, "concerns itself with my eccentric and, sometimes, tragic pals."

About the Contributing Journals

The Capilano Review has been published out of Capilano College's Humanities Division since 1972. It is a tri-annual magazine of the arts, publishing poetry, fiction, fine art, and drama from all over Canada and the world. It has been recognized for excellence five times by the National Magazine Awards and been cited by the Canadian Studies Association. Its distribution spans nine countries. Subscriptions are $25 for one year (three issues). Write to *The Capilano Review* c/o Capilano College, 2055 Purcell Way, North Vancouver, B.C., v7j 3h5. Telephone: (604) 984-1712, Fax: (604) 983-7520.

Exile is a quarterly magazine which features Canadian fiction and poetry as well as the work of writers in translation from all over the world; some the best-known, others unknown. Publisher and Editor: Barry Callaghan. Submissions and correspondence: Box 67, Station B, Toronto, Ontario, m5t 2c0.

Grain "Food For Your Brain" magazine provides readers with fine, fresh writing by new and established writers of poetry and prose, four times a year. Published by the Saskatchewan Writers Guild, *Grain* has earned national and international recognition for its distinctive literary content. Editor: J. Jill Robinson. Prose Editor: Connie Gault. Poetry Editor: Tim Lilburn. Submissions and correspondence: Box 1154, Regina, Saskatchewan, s4p 3b4. E-mail: grain.mag@sasknet.sk.ca Web site: http://www.sasknet.com/corporate/skwriter

The Malahat Review publishes mostly fiction and poetry and includes a substantial review article in each issue. It is open to dramatic works, so long as they lend themselves to the page; it welcomes literary works that defy easy generic categorization. Editor: Derk Wynard. Associate Editor: Marlene Cookshaw.

Assistant Editor: Lucy Bashford. Submissions and correspondence: University of Victoria, P.O. Box 1700, MS 8524, Victoria, B.C., v8w 2Y2.

The New Quarterly promotes new writers and new kinds of writing with a special interest in work which stretches the bounds of realism. It publishes poetry, short fiction, essays on writing, and interviews with occasional special issues on themes and genres in Canadian writing. Submissions and correspondence: c/o ELPP, PAS 2082, University of Waterloo, Waterloo, Ontario, N2L 3G1.

Other Voices is an Edmonton-based literary magazine which publishes two issues a year. It considers high quality work from any perspective, from both new and established writers, particularly women. Its editors are interested primarily in fiction and non-fiction prose and poetry, but also welcome reviews and artwork. Submissions and correspondence: P.O. Box 52059, 8210–109 Street, Edmonton, Alberta, T6G 2T5.

Prairie Fire is a quarterly magazine of contemporary Canadian writing which regularly publishes stories, poems, book reviews, and visual art by emerging as well as established writers and artists. *Prairie Fire*'s editorial mix also occasionally features critical and personal essays, interviews with authors, and readers' letters. *Prairie Fire* publishes a fiction issue every summer. Some of *Prairie Fire*'s most popular issues have been double-sized editions on multicultural themes, individual authors, and different genres. *Prairie Fire* publishes writing from, and has readers in, virtually all parts of Canada. Editor: Andris Taskans; Fiction editors: Heidi Harms, Susan Rempel Letkemann and Joan Thomas. Submissions and correspondence: Rm. 423–100 Arthur Street, Winnipeg, Manitoba, R3B 1H3.

Prism international has published, for more than thirty years, work by writers both new and established, Canadian and international. Edited by graduate students of creative writing at the University of British Columbia, *Prism* looks for innovative fiction, poetry, drama, as well as creative non-fiction, in English or English translation. The 1996/7 editorial board will consist of, in part, Sara O'Leary as Editor and Tim Mitchell as Executive Editor. *Prism* also holds an annual fiction contest. Request guidelines or send submissions to: The Editors, *Prism international*, Department of Creative Writing, BUCH E462–1866 Main Mall, University of British Columbia, Vancouver, B.C., v6T 1z1. E-mail: prism@unixg.ubc.ca Web site: http://www.arts.ubc.ca/crwr/prism/prism.html

Queen's Quarterly, founded in 1893, is the oldest intellectual journal in Canada. It publishes articles on a variety of subjects and consequently fiction occupies relatively little space. There are one or two stories in each issue. However, because of its lively format and eclectic mix of subject matter, *Queen's Quarterly* attracts readers with widely diverse interests. This exposure is an advantage many of our fiction writers appreciate. Submissions are welcome from both new and established writers. Fiction Editor: Joan Harcourt. Submissions and correspondence: Queen's University, Kingston, Ontario, K7L 3N6.

Windsor Review is a biannual periodical committed to publishing original short fiction, poetry, essays, and reviews. It is a literary journal that publishes the creative and critical work of both young and experienced artists and scholars. Fiction Editor: Alistair MacLeod. Submissions and correspondence: The Department of English, University of Windsor, 401 Sunset Avenue, Windsor, Ontario, N9B 3P4.

WRIT Magazine, a literary annual of poetry, fiction, and translation, has been published in Toronto since 1970. It has now ceased publication except for a special issue planned for Spring 1997; unsolicited manuscripts should therefore no longer be sent to WRIT.

Submissions were received from the following journals:

The Antigonish Review
(Antigonish, N.S.)

Parchment
(North York, Ont.)

Blood & Aphorisms
(Toronto, Ont.)

Pottersfield Portfolio
(Halifax, N.S.)

Dalhousie Review
(Halifax, N.S.)

Quarry Magazine
(Kingston, Ont.)

Event
(New Westminster, B.C.)

Storyteller
(Kanata, Ont.)

The Fiddlehead
(Fredericton, N.B.)

TickleAce
(St. John's, Nfld.)

Green's Magazine
(Regina, Sask.)

The Toronto Review
(Toronto, Ont.)

ink magazine
(Toronto, Ont.)

White Wall Review
(Toronto, Ont.)

Kairos
(Hamilton, Ont.)

The Journey Prize Anthology
List of Previous Contributing Authors

* Winners of the $10,000 Journey Prize

1

1989

Ven Begamudré, "Word Games"
David Bergen, "Where You're From"
Lois Braun, "The Pumpkin-Eaters"
Constance Buchanan, "Man with Flying Genitals"
Ann Copeland, "Obedience"
Marion Douglas, "Flags"
Frances Itani, "An Evening in the Café"
Diane Keating, "The Crying Out"
Thomas King, "One Good Story, That One"
Holley Rubinsky, "Rapid Transits"*
Jean Rysstad, "Winter Baby"
Kevin Van Tighem, "Whoopers"
M.G. Vassanji, "In the Quiet of a Sunday Afternoon"
Bronwen Wallace, "Chicken 'N' Ribs"
Armin Wiebe, "Mouse Lake"
Budge Wilson, "Waiting"

2

1990

André Alexis, "Despair: Five Stories of Ottawa"
Glen Allen, "The Hua Guofeng Memorial Warehouse"
Marusia Bociurkiw, "Mama, Donya"
Virgil Burnett, "Billfrith the Dreamer"
Margaret Dyment, "Sacred Trust"
Cynthia Flood, "My Father Took a Cake to France"*
Douglas Glover, "Story Carved in Stone"
Terry Griggs, "Man with the Axe"

Rick Hillis, "Limbo River"
Thomas King, "The Dog I Wish I Had, I Would Call It Helen"
K.D. Miller, "Sunrise Till Dark"
Jennifer Mitton, "Let Them Say"
Lawrence O'Toole, "Goin' to Town with Katie Ann"
Kenneth Radu, "A Change of Heart"
Jenifer Sutherland, "Table Talk"
Wayne Tefs, "Red Rock and After"

3
1991

Donald Aker, "The Invitation"
Anton Baer, "Yukon"
Allan Barr, "A Visit from Lloyd"
David Bergen, "The Fall"
Rai Berzins, "Common Sense"
Diana Hartog, "Theories of Grief"
Diane Keating, "The Salem Letters"
Yann Martel, "The Facts Behind the Helsinki Roccamatios"*
Jennifer Mitton, "Polaroid"
Sheldon Oberman, "This Business with Elijah"
Lynn Podgurny, "Till Tomorrow, Maple Leaf Mills"
James Riseborough, "She Is Not His Mother"
Patricia Stone, "Living on the Lake"

4
1992

David Bergen, "The Bottom of the Glass"
Maria A. Billion, "No Miracles Sweet Jesus"
Judith Cowan, "By the Big River"
Steven Heighton, "A Man Away from Home Has No Neighbours"
Steven Heighton, "How Beautiful upon the Mountains"
L. Rex Kay, "Travelling"
Rozena Maart, "No Rosa, No District Six"*
Guy Malet De Carteret, "Rainy Day"
Carmelita McGrath, "Silence"
Michael Mirolla, "A Theory of Discontinuous Existence"

Diane Juttner Perreault, "Bella's Story"
Eden Robinson, "Traplines"

5
1993

Caroline Adderson, "Oil and Dread"
David Bergen, "La Rue Prevette"
Marina Endicott, "With the Band"
Dayv James-French, "Cervine"
Michael Kenyon, "Durable Tumblers"
K.D. Miller, "A Litany in Time of Plague"
Robert Mullen, "Flotsam"
Gayla Reid, "Sister Doyle's Men"*
Oakland Ross, "Bang-bang"
Robert Sherrin, "Technical Battle for Trial Machine"
Carol Windley, "The Etruscans"

6
1994

Anne Carson, "Water Margins: An Essay on Swimming by
    My Brother"
Richard Cumyn, "The Sound He Made"
Genni Gunn, "Versions"
Melissa Hardy, "Long Man the River"*
Robert Mullen, "Anomie"
Vivian Payne, "Free Falls"
Jim Reil, "Dry"
Robyn Sarah, "Accept My Story"
Joan Skogan, "Landfall"
Dorothy Speak, "Relatives in Florida"
Alison Wearing, "Notes from Under Water"

7
1995

Michelle Alfano, "Opera"
Mary Borsky, "Maps of the Known World"
Gabriella Goliger, "Song of Ascent"

Elizabeth Hay, "Hand Games"
Shaena Lambert, "The Falling Woman"
Elise Levine, "Boy"
Roger Burford Mason, "The Rat-Catcher's Kiss"
Antanas Sileika, "Going Native"
Kathryn Woodward, "Of Marranos and Gilded Angels"*